A WHALE OF THE WILD

A WHALE OF THE WILD

ROSANNE PARRY

ILLUSTRATIONS BY
LINDSAY MOORE

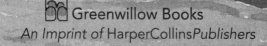

Greenwillow Books
An Imprint of HarperCollinsPublishers

Thank you to Katie Jones at the Center for Whale Research, for answering my questions about orcas. I also want to acknowledge The Whale Museum for their wonderful educational displays and the SeaDoc Society for all the information and outreach they provide to the public about the Salish Sea. And thank you to Rosanne Parry for writing a beautiful story about orcas, something my ten-year-old self would have dreamed to illustrate.—Lindsay Moore

A Whale of the Wild
Text copyright © 2020 by Rosanne Parry
Illustrations copyright © 2020 by Lindsay Moore
Back matter orca photographs © Ken Rea, Spirit of Orca; orca tooth photograph courtesy of Tracie Merrill, The Whale Museum, Friday Harbor, Washington
Map by Elizabeth Person
Special thanks to Katie Jones of the Center for Whale Research for her expert fact-checking

The text of this book is set in Berling.
Book design by Sylvie Le Floc'h

Library of Congress Control Number: 2020941144

ISBN 978-0-06-299592-6 (hardback)

20 21 22 23 24 PC/LSCH 10 9 8 7 6 5 4 3 2
First Edition

 Greenwillow Books

For Monica, my matriarch in the making,
and for all our future wayfinders and faithful followers

Contents

≈

➤ ➤ ➤

A WHALE OF THE WILD

CHAPTER ONE
KINSHIP

In the early morning before the wind of the day wakes up, before the Push of the tide changes to the Pull, there is nothing to stir the mist that floats above the water. Nothing but me.

My family is sleeping, all rising and breathing together after a weary night of searching for, and not finding, salmon. I swim beside them and roll belly up, just below the surface. Each beat of my flukes makes a ring of ripples on the still water. The ripples nudge the mist. It swirls up and away from my path as if I am some giant thing, a rising tide or a storm wind.

I am not so big. Not yet. For now, I am just a daughter—not strong enough to be a savvy hunter like Mother, nor wise enough to be a master wayfinder like Greatmother. I am not old enough to be a mother like my cousin Aquila, and not young enough to delight my family like the younglings do with their games and sweet chirping voices. They say I will be a brilliant wayfinder someday. But I cannot imagine them following me.

When I am dancing with the mist of early morning, I do not care. I roll again and let my fin break through the skin of the sea and split the fog in two. I huff a great *chaaaah* out of the breather on top of my head. The sun lifts above the ridge of mountains, casting a golden glow across the Salish Sea. I turn downward, darkward, gathering speed, and then lift my head skyward. I beat my flukes hard against the grip of the earth and the weight of water, tucking my flippers close to my sides. I burst into the air and imagine myself turning into a raven and soaring among the clouds. I arch over and hit the water with a satisfying smack and a happy fizz of bubbles. When I rise to the surface again, Greatmother is there, watching me.

"Beauty is the food of the mind," she says.

Wayfinders are like this. They say nonsensical things. I was trying to forget about food. I was hoping to want it less. But now Greatmother has reminded me, and my hunger comes roaring back like a winter storm.

"Eat a little beauty every day, my Vega, my bright star," Greatmother says. She comes over to nuzzle me. "It will give you strength."

That makes no sense at all! is the thing I do not say out loud. Nobody questions the wayfinder. We follow. Always. But while the rest of my family is waking up, I chase the last wisps of fog and bite into them. Just in case. They are nothing but a drizzle of rain on my tongue.

We gather around Mother and Greatmother, shaking off sleep, ready to follow them.

"Our Chinooks will return to us," Greatmother says firmly. "They always have. Since the time of ice."

She leads us on, choosing a path around the islands and inlets of our home waters. Mother travels shoulder to shoulder with her. Mother is the wisest of hunters. If she cannot find our salmon, no one can. And none of us needs our salmon more. Her belly is broader every day. When I make a click-stream, I can see the shape of my soon-to-be-born sister inside her. It has been a hard year, a lean year. But babies are always good luck, and she is the sister I have been waiting for my whole life.

We fall into our usual places. Greatmother leads us. Mother nudges the younglings, Deneb and Altair, to the middle, where they can be well looked after. Uncle Rigel swims on one side of them, Aquila on the other. I do not have a particular spot, so I tag along behind where I can hear and see everybody, but they will not pay attention to me.

We are a thing to see when we travel. One fin after another cuts through the water, rising like an ocean wave, fast and sleek and strong. Sharks head for the shadows when we come around. Eels slide farther into their caves. Gulls scatter. Seals watch us from their resting spots with wide brown eyes.

All day long Mother sends her click-stream into shallows and under stone arches. She circles underwater rock spires and forest-covered islands, looking for our salmon. We all search. The sea is full of fish, but none are big enough, meaty enough, rich enough. None are salmon. Pull changes over to Push. The younglings are ready to eat anything that moves.

"Fish! Fish! Fish!" Altair chants while Deneb flushes out one of the spiky fellows hiding in the rocks. I have already learned my lesson about those. I am not surprised a moment later to see the youngling boys spitting out the pointy bits and finding not much left to swallow.

I cannot blame them. Another long day of hunting, another day of hunger. The sun is going down by the time we come to a less rocky spot with a smooth bottom. I spy a pair of eyes in the mud—blinking. I stop my bubble stream and draw in a mouthful of water. You can never tell how big a fish is from the size of the eyes. In my imagination, this one is big enough to feed us all. I squirt the water out of my mouth. It lifts the fish from the mud, and in one snap I have him! I crunch down until I hear the middle bone crack. Every fish has a middle bone, and when you break it, they stop fighting. I shake off the mud and sand.

It is small. Barely a mouthful. I blow out a big sad bubble and rise for breath. Deneb spies my catch first, and Altair is right beside him.

"Share! Share!"

These are the first words a baby learns. We alone among the creatures of the sea share our food.

"My clever Vega!" Mother says. "Always noticing

the little things. It takes a sharp eye to find a flat fish."

We all know that flat fish are flavorless. Not quite as unsatisfying as eating clouds, but almost.

"Only a little one," I say.

I offer her the first bite. She shares her half, so I do the same. The piece I'm left with is hardly worth swallowing. I wish I had given the whole thing to Mother. She needs every mouthful she can get. I look through Mother's belly to see the curled shape of my baby sister.

"She is growing just as she should," Mother says. "I promise."

It is not kind to look through someone, but I cannot stop checking on Capella. I rub my head ever so gently across the stretched skin of Mother's belly. A sister, a sister of my own! Someone to love and look after. Someone to swim at my side and share the work of a wayfinder.

⫸ ⫸ ⫸

Greatmother takes us out of the shallow and silty inlet to a place where the island is steep sided and rocky. The Push is stronger here. We rest and let it carry us along. There is a cave at the waterline that I remember from the last time we came this way. I move closer, and just like last time, there is a mother seal and her baby asleep inside. Another seal is floating just outside the cave, crunching through the skin of one of the spiny fishes without a flinch. Maybe it would not be so bad to eat a prickly one. I am hungry enough to try.

I duck under the water and send out my click-stream. I wait for the echo of my clicks to return, tilting my chin up to catch even the faintest sound.

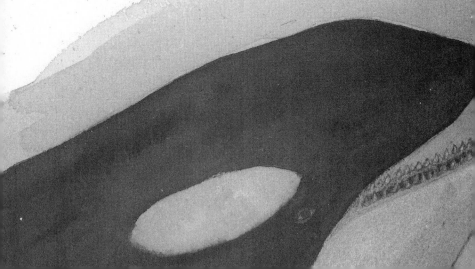

My clicks show me the cracks and crevices where fish like to hide, as if sunlight could reach there. I see a few of the prickly fellows and then . . . a big flash of silver.

I quick turn. Click-stream again. Yes, oh yes! Smooth sides all speckled gray, a hooked mouth, and fast!

A salmon! A Silver!

I surge forward and it swerves toward the rocks, looking for a niche too narrow for my teeth to

follow. I keep after it, and it zigzags up the face of the cliff. It jumps into the air. I scrape my side on the rocks in pursuit. I can taste it already. I snap and miss. It jumps again. I gather my strength and leap. I cannot quite grab it from the air, but with a swing of my head I knock it against the side of the cliff. It falls back into the water, stunned. I grab it, pushing my teeth deep into its meaty sides. Salmon! At last!

For a moment, I just hold the salmon in my teeth and breathe out round bubbles of bliss. I caught it all by myself! A Silver—not quite as mighty as our kings, our Chinooks, but food, real food. I feel that burst of oily goodness in my mouth. It is mine! All mine. I could eat it in one bite.

My family is ahead, turning in to the next passage between islands. They would never know I did not share it. I take a nibble. It is as rich as I remember.

I lift my head out of the water and watch my family swimming all together under the stars. One after another they breathe out a spray of air, water, and salt. Tall breaths from Mother and

Greatmother; medium sized from Aquila, who is only twenty seasons older than me. Old Uncle Rigel has the biggest breaths of all. The smallest spouts come from the younglings—my brother, Deneb, and Aquila's baby, Altair.

They are about to move around a bend where they will not be able to see me with even the strongest click-stream or hear me if I call. My heart races. I have never been alone before. I could get away with eating my entire salmon and then catch up. I could. My stomach makes a happy gurgle at the thought.

And then Uncle Rigel's big fin turns, and I feel his click-stream wash over me. Mother calls my name, and then Greatmother and Aquila too. They are all hungry. Every one of them. Still, they are waiting. For me.

In the space of one heartbeat, my greed is unthinkable. A little together is more than a feast alone. So much more! I carry my salmon to them and we share. It is not enough. Not even close, but we are together, whatever the Push and Pull of the tides will bring.

CHAPTER TWO
NOISE

Vega caught a salmon! A big one! Well, medium big. I leap right over her to celebrate. She holds it in her teeth, and I take my bite. It's been a whole season since we've found a Silver. Everyone says they're not as good as the Chinooks, but I'm too hungry to care.

"Well hunted," Mother says.

"It's not easy to catch one all on your own," Greatmother adds.

"How did you find it?"

"Well . . ."

Vega looks

a little flustered. I'm glad I don't have to answer to Greatmother like my sister does. She's so much braver than me.

"I saw a cliff face with crevices. Prickly fish like to hide, so I thought a salmon might hide there too. I did not know for sure if I would find one," Vega adds. "I guessed."

Greatmother gives a rare nod of approval.

"It's time," Mother says proudly. "You can think like a hunter. Come lead us like a wayfinder."

I see a flush of pink all down Vega's white belly.

"Time indeed," Greatmother says. She nudges Vega into the wayfinder's position. That's never happened before. Sometimes Aquila leads when we're in an easy stretch of water. I thought Vega would be much older before it was her turn.

I see a shiver of power go through Vega. She's ready!

"Are you sure?" she says, because a wayfinder never brags.

"We learn to lead by trying," says Mother. "And

by trusting each other. You know the way."

"Your name star is at the top of the sky," Greatmother says solemnly. "Salmon season is upon us. Our kinship will be gathering."

"I know the way," Aquila says eagerly. "The Gathering Place is warmward, past this island and the next one. . . ."

She goes on and on. Aquila knows everything. She is constantly at Greatmother's side, and she always has the right answer. And she always interrupts when it's Vega's turn to talk. I could bite her!

I start to sneak over to Aquila, but Uncle Rigel heads me off. He puffs out a big warning bubble right under my chin. I don't know how such an old guy can move so fast. I veer away and give Vega a chirp of encouragement instead.

"I can find the way," Vega says.

She's going to lead the way! I jump-spin-splash. I swim a circle around her, smacking my flukes on the water to announce to even the littlest fish that my sister—my Vega—will take the lead today. And she's only forty-four seasons old—a legend already!

I get in place to be her first follower. Also, I'm ready to bite Aquila's fluke if she does something bossy.

"Lead on," Mother says.

Vega sweeps the waters ahead with her click-stream, even though I know she has everything memorized. She has a story for each kelp forest and funny-shaped rock. She knows where the net boats are and how to not get tangled in them. There are lots of paths through the Middle Islands that could take us to the Gathering Place. Vega will choose the best one. The one with fish to eat. As we set off, Aquila and Mother sing "Side by Side and Fin by Fluke" to Altair, to encourage him to stay close, just like they used to sing to me when I was small.

I listen to Vega tell herself the story of each sea mark as we come to it—the steep slope with the ledge of bird nests . . . the rocky point with the lightning-struck tree . . . the sunken boat with all the eels lurking inside. I repeat every way marker as she calls them out. She's going to lead our kinship when she's old. And me? I'm going to have a fin as tall as Uncle Rigel's and a wicked scar on my back just like his, proof of my brave deeds.

Ahead is an open passage between the steep-sided island and the island with the shallower slope where the water runs as fast as the wind. Vega lets us rest for a moment as she looks all around.

"The Push is strong here," she calls out. "But easier waters lie ahead." She encourages us, like wayfinders do.

As we round the end of the island and move into open water, the terrible roar of a human carrier reaches us. The noise is so loud it makes

everything dark. I put my head above the water to escape the sound. The churning growlers are coming right toward us. Why did Vega take us this way? We have to get out of here!

My heart races. Vega's going to lead us in a different direction. I'm sure of it. She was bitten by a boat's growler six seasons ago. There's still a notch on her fin. She hates the big boats.

Vega hovers, completely still. I can't stop shaking, but she doesn't even flinch! So brave! She definitely has a plan. We could backtrack and go the long way around. I'm tired, but I will follow her anywhere.

Vega looks at Mother, click-streaming through her skin to see the baby. Mother is much more tired than me. The long way around will be hard for her. But I'll help. She can swim in my shadow when she gets tired. I look to Vega for the signal to turn back.

The lights of the human carrier shine out in all directions. The honk of its horn is louder than a whole colony of long-nosed seals. We have to get out of here now!

"Come on!" Vega calls. "Stay close." She plunges into the passage, ahead of the human carrier.

For a moment we all pause, trying to understand why she would risk the growlers of the human carrier. But she's my sister—my wayfinder—and I'm the first to follow her.

"Coming!" I shout to Vega over the noise. She knows we can cross in time. Why else would she take the chance? I wince against the pounding noise and swim to her side. Our family follows.

Vega tries to hurry, but little Altair can only go so fast, even with Aquila nudging him along. I send out my click-stream to help light our way, but the noise drowns my clicks and darkness falls around me.

I think I hear Vega shouting.

"Turn back!" Or maybe it's "Try harder!"

I spin around and around, but I can't see my family or even feel them moving beside me. The growlers thrash great clouds of bubbles into the water. The human carrier is nearly on top of us. Again I hear shouting, but I can't tell what I should

do. I reach out
my flippers. I know
my family is close, but in the
noise it feels like they're an ocean away. All I can
hear is my own heart racing.

Then out of the darkness Mother and
Greatmother appear, swimming close enough to
touch me. I lean into them, shivering with relief.
I'm aching to rise for breath, but the boat is too
close. I squeeze my breather tight and wait. Mother

and Greatmother join their click-streams together. A faint glimmer of the path ahead shines out. I swim in the shadow of the strongest wayfinders of my kinship.

They take us under the boat. Vega shivers as she swims beside me, even though we are well clear of the biting teeth on the back end. I feel the pressure of it passing above. I gather my strength and swim faster, away from the growlers, away from the groan-rattle-thrum, out of the passage between islands and into the shallows of a protected cove. I plunge into the tall thin trunks of a kelp forest, gasping for breath.

The heat of my panic drains away and in time the shivering stops. I am cold and ashamed. Vega led us wrong. How could she?

"That was too close!" I shout. "Why did you do it?"

A breath later I regret it. Who am I to question a wayfinder? Uncle Rigel never would. It was her first try. Vega's heart is racing just as fast as mine. Mother and Greatmother go among us, soothing our fears and praising our courage.

Nobody speaks to Vega. She holds herself apart from us.

We rest together in the cove, dozing and waking and dozing again. The smooth flat fronds of kelp stroke our

sides, and the steady roll of the waves rocks us. Just before the sun rises, Greatmother leads us out of the kelp and into open water. But when she turns oceanward and heads for the Gathering Place, Vega turns in the other direction and swims away.

Alone.

I can't believe it. Two wrong things in one night!

Should I tell Mother? Should I not tell? Everyone has their eyes on Greatmother. They can't even imagine leaving the family.

I can imagine it. My heart goes chasing after my sister, but the whole rest of my body sticks to my place. I know where I belong. Still, it feels like I'm being torn in two.

CHAPTER THREE
BIRDS

I led them wrong. How could I have chosen so badly?

The bone-shaking noise of the human carrier is still in my ears. My heart is still pounding. I was sure I could get past it, but it was going faster than I thought. And Altair was so slow.

What if Mother or baby Capella had gotten hurt? They are better off without me. Aquila is the one they need. She will be a perfect wayfinder someday.

The sea stretches before me, and I click-stream down into the dark water, searching for salmon to eat. In the returning echoes I see the rocky slope of the bottom. A seal and her baby, all chubby and sleek, dodge away from me as if they know what I have done.

"I am Vega, daughter of Arctura, greatdaughter of Siria, of the Warmward Kinship of Salmon Eaters," I announce to them. The mother turns to blink at me and waggle her sparse whiskers.

"I am not the kind of orca who eats you," I add in a spirit of fellowship. But the seal turns back to her baby and swims away.

A solitary octopus slithers along the rocky slope. It dodges away from an eel's cave in a graceful swirl of tentacles. The eel lurks in her rocky cavern, all teeth and patience. I consider giving them a proper greeting. But the unfriendliness of eels and octopuses is in all the stories, so I leave them alone.

If I could find salmon for my family, then I would deserve to travel with them. But salmon are not to be found, and hunger is like a stone in me. Still, I keep searching. A salmon has to eat. Out in the ocean in the cold season I saw them gobbling up all kinds of little fishes. I change my strategy.

Find the salmon food, find the salmon, I tell myself.

I reshape my click-stream to search for the feeder fish our salmon eat when we are in the ocean. I head for a shallower place. As I approach, I see a green cloud. A swarm of little creatures come to feed on the green cloud. They are too small to see, but I can hear the snap and crackle of a thousand tiny mouths eating. I see the silver flicker of smelt and herring darting through the green cloud to snap up the invisible creatures. More little fish come, and still more, until the water shimmers like a starry sky. And now bigger hunters come.

Murres and puffins gather first. Murres are the great fish herders of the sea. They are black on their backs and white on their bellies, just like me. They are duck sized, and in the air they are the clumsiest birds I have ever seen. But underwater they are silent and deadly. Nobody can turn and swoop and dodge like them. Sometimes I go to the shallow spots just to watch them hunt.

The murres swim around the tiny fishes, banking and gliding in ever smaller circles. They drive them into a bunch, a shimmering moon of fish. The murres pick off the herring from the edges, grabbing them by their tails and swallowing them whole. Surely salmon will come to a feast like this. How could they resist? I lurk in the shadows and wait.

Gulls fly in next. They sit on the skin of the sea. They dangle their triangles and reach down to snap up fish. I search all around for salmon, but none come to take their share. I am so intent on the task that I do not even notice the whale until it is right underneath me.

It is a gulper whale, a little minke. It approaches from below and lunges upward, mouth open. Its throat billows out and fills with water and fish. The whale closes its mouth and sinks back; its tongue pushes out the water. It swallows the squirming lump of fish that remain.

I pity the gulper whales, especially these little ones. They have no proper teeth, just a mouth fringe to strain their tiny meals from the water. Their blows are half-hearted; their flippers are laughably small. Clearly, inside and out, I am the superior sea creature. And yet the minke has a mouth full of food, while I, for all my prowess, am as empty as a jellyfish.

The minke swims away, leaving behind a cloudy streak that shimmers with fish scales. The murres go back to the work of fish roundup. Puffins join

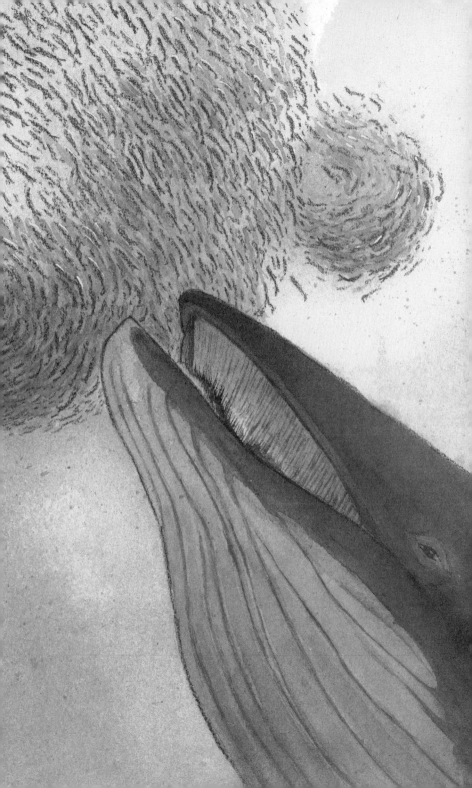

them, their thick orange beaks snapping up many fish at one go.

"We do not eat herring," I have been told more than once. "Respect the fish our salmon need," Greatmother always says. "If you eat everything, you make a wasteland of the sea."

Still, I am hungry. And nobody is watching.

I position myself under the swirling moon of fish. I turn skyward, pump my flukes, and open my mouth. Water and fish fall in as I swim upward. When I break into open air, I snap my teeth together and discover, to my shock, that I have caught a gull by the triangle. I try the whale's trick of pushing the water out with my tongue, only to see most of the little fish escape. But not the gull. It stays stubbornly lodged between my teeth. It flaps madly against the tender spots on my chin. I gulp down the fish still in my mouth and lift my head into the air. The gull screams and beats its wings against my face, even harder than before. I give it a helpful shake to loosen it, and it only screams louder.

"Vega, daughter of Arctura, let that bird go!" Aquila shouts.

I spin to face my cousin. Caught again! Doing something foolish. Again!

"Mmph!" I mumble, working the stuck triangle with my tongue. The gull is losing its strength to fight. I keep it carefully above the water.

"We do not eat birds," Aquila says. "Honestly, Vega, you have known this for ages." She huffs out an impatient breath. "It's not hard to remember, not even for you."

I concentrate on pushing the gull's triangle with my tongue, sliding it down the length of my teeth.

"It's not right! It's not dignified," Aquila goes on. And on.

I stop listening, but her words strike hard, like the frozen rain of winter.

"How are you going to learn it all? There's so much to remember! You have to try harder than this."

I will never be good enough.

"I need you to try, Vega. Why won't you even try?"

I do try. Every day. But Aquila only sees when I do it wrong. I keep working to help the gull. It is not flapping at all now.

"What will become of us?" Aquila says more softly. "Why can't you be more like your mother?"

When the gull is finally free, I nudge it, beak side up, onto the skin of the sea. "Don't sink," I whistle quietly. "Please don't sink."

"Are you listening?" Aquila says. "You swam away! What's the matter with you?" She click-streams me fiercely, looking right through to where the herrings are sloshing unpleasantly inside me.

I hate being looked through. And Aquila does it to me all the time. I wish I could find an orca-sized cave to hide in like an eel.

Aquila glares up at the poor gull, still struggling to swim away. I give it a gentle nudge. The gull paddles and flaps. I offer another nudge, and then one more. I regret so much.

"Let me look at you now," Aquila says, switching to her motherly tone. She clicks gently over my head. "Did the bird hurt you?"

"No," I mumble.

I glance around, suddenly aware that we are

alone. Altair has never left Aquila's side, not since the day he was born. I look again. Where could he be? For a moment I think the worst, but no. Aquila would be sick with grief if Altair were lost. But she is fine. A little crabby. Disappointed in me, as usual. She left him behind with the others. Left him to find me.

I am pleased but ashamed, too. We used to be best friends. All the games of tag and hide-and-seek and jump the fin—I miss them. But Aquila is a mother now, and there is no pushing back the sun. She is too old for games, and I am too stubborn to give them up. But when Capella is born, then I will have a sister of my own to guard and play with. She will need me.

"Don't worry," I mumble. "I won't do it again. I was just—"

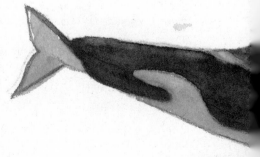

"—Hungry?" Aquila says. She gives me a nuzzle like she used to.

I blow a big sad bubble.

"Me too," Aquila says. "And I think I know where to find salmon. Will you hunt with me? It's the new game, Vega. It's a better game. And we have our whole lives to play it together. Will you come? Our family needs you."

I do not believe her, not in my heart, but what else can I do? I slide into Aquila's swim shadow and we head for the Gathering Place together, side by side and fin by fluke.

CHAPTER FOUR
GATHERING

I follow Aquila. Not because I want to. I follow her because when I send out my click-stream as far as I can make it go, I do not see my family. Not even a fleeting shadow of them. They could be anywhere. There are stories of younglings who got lost and even whole families who disappeared and were never found again. I do not say that I am frightened. Aquila would never leave her baby unless she knew how to find him again. But I do swim close enough to touch her.

When I was younger, I was always measuring myself against my cousin—height of fin, length of flipper. I was so eager to catch up. Today I am relieved to see her fin taller than mine. Glad I still have time to grow. We swim side by side, flippers touching, playing our old game of seeing how long we can hold the connection.

"You know," Aquila says. "We could be the first ones to find our Chinooks."

"They must be close," I say. "The summer stars are in place. The kinship is gathering."

Mountains mark the edge of the Salish Sea like a great reef on the land. They have called the

salmon out of the ocean for as long as our kinship can remember. Nobody knows exactly how the mountains speak to the salmon, but every year rains fall in their forests and rush down in rivers and streams, pushing great plumes of gray and turquoise water into the sea. Salmon hear that call and come home from the vast ocean, feeding us on the way.

When the seasons turn again, tiny salmon whoosh out of the rivers and streams, all speckled and silver like their parents. They hide in the eelgrass prairies until they are big enough to swim out into the open ocean. And then they vanish into the Blue

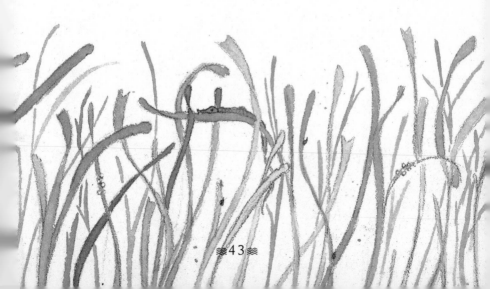

Wilderness, where none of our kinship dares to go. But the mountains are faithful, and the seasons turn again. Rain falls. Mountains call their salmon home. One big circle, like the long dance we make with our whole family every salmon season.

I savor the thought of being the first to find a run of salmon, not one fish, but a kinship of them as big as a storm cloud. I want to be the first to sink my teeth in, the first to share. I am hungry not just for the feeling of a full belly. I am hungry to know that our mountains have not forgotten us. Hungry to know that our salmon have survived the Blue Wilderness and remembered their way home.

Aquila and I swim toward the setting sun. We sweep the sea with our click-streams. We click louder when boats are near.

"A little farther," Aquila says cheerfully.

We watch porpoises content themselves with the smelt and herring, and we keep going.

Below us, a gray whale is making its dull *thunk-a-thunk-a-thunk* call as it scoops its boring food out of the muck on the sea bottom. And we keep going.

"Almost there," Aquila says, just as cheerful as before.

"Over here now."

"Just beyond that sandbar."

"After the thing carrier passes."

She is tenacious. And cheerful. It is getting on my nerves. Even sea stars and brainless urchins are chomping and chewing away.

When I was a youngling, I thought Greatmother knew the sea down to its last drop. I thought she and Mother and all the greatmothers of my kinship were the ones to call salmon out of the ocean. But the more I learn, the more questions I have. Sometimes there are so many seals and sea lions that battles are fought over our salmon. Sometimes net boats come and take from us. Some seasons our salmon run strong, and there is enough

for everyone. Sometimes the salmon come late or only a few make it home. No one can say why.

I move with her toward the deeper part of the passage and feel a little thrill as the bottom drops out of sight. I love depths! I am not especially fond of the spiky crabs who side-walk around down there on all those legs. Squid, also not my favorite. Again, too many legs. But I love to tell spooky stories about what lurks beyond the reach of sunlight— the same stories that Aquila told me when I was young enough to believe she knew everything. Some of the stories were so scary we would both hide under our mothers' flippers afterward.

Mother would make her comforting thrums. "Nothing hunts us," she would remind me.

But Greatmother always said, "There are more things in the ocean than even I have seen."

I love to imagine what fearsome creatures lurk in the depths, unseen for hundreds of seasons. I long to discover what no one in my kinship has

ever seen, to find something so tiny that we have overlooked it, or so deep that it lives by a glow of its own making.

On the shore just ahead I can see piles of rectangles and streams of land boats—the roosting spot of a huge flock of humans. Our gathering place is on the far side of this human roost. Two seamounts, tall and slender, mark the spot. All the families of my kinship have come here to watch the salmon return for as long as the greatmothers can remember.

The faint taste of saltier water from the ocean reminds me of winter days spent along the stormy coasts. We are close to the Gathering Place now. When I send out my click-stream, I can see the faint shadow of many orcas all swimming together ahead. I cannot wait to be with them after the long season apart. I call out to them.

Before they can answer, a power of the earth shakes the very stones of the sea. The first jolt hits like the punch of lightning into water.

"What was that?" I shout, turning toward Aquila.

She swims to my side and tucks me under her flippers like I am her own baby. Another jolt! A low grinding sound so loud I can feel it on my skin. Little sand hiders and bottom fish float up from their hiding places and hang in the water, too shocked to swim away. Bubbles whoosh upward as if some monstrous thing is breathing under the bottom of the sea. The water has a sudden bitter tang.

I hide in Aquila's shadow, afraid to come up for air. The bubbles stop rising as abruptly as they began. And the grinding of rock against rock stops a moment later. Aquila and I rise side by side for a breath, a breath, and another.

"It is a power of the earth," Aquila says.

She sounds as shaky as I feel. Fish hang in the water, stunned. Little sea shakes happen sometimes. I have felt them before. But this one

sounded different.
And I have never
seen bubbles come
out of the bottom
of the sea.

"The earth itches,
just as we do." Aquila
recites the story
Greatmother told us
both when we were small.
"It rolls and rubs against
rock as we do and sometimes
bits of it break free, just like
we shed old skin."

There is a pleading to
her voice. She needs me to
believe the story so she
can too. I am not sure
what I believe, but a
familiar ache in my
chest prompts me

to breathe. Above water, everything looks the same. Eagles soar. Boats churn this way and that. Ashore, among the piles of rectangles, little land boats roll along like always.

"We should keep going," I say. "Altair will be frightened."

Aquila agrees before I have a chance to say, *Deneb too*. My brother acts brave, but he is only twenty seasons old. I was wrong to leave him.

We have not gone far when Greatmother's call reaches us.

"I am Siria of the Warmward Kinship of Great Salmon Eaters."

"I am Arctura, daughter of Siria," Mother calls after her.

"Me! I am me!" Altair squeaks, eager to join the game and all out of turn.

I leap for joy. My family!

Others call out their names. Mothers and sisters first and then brothers and sons. Except for Altair, who chirps "Me! Me!" nonstop. I hear my mother's sister, Aunt Nova, and Greatmother's two older sisters. Their daughters and sons call out. I check their names against my memory. Are they all here?

A few moments later and much farther away, I hear the other voices of my kinship still traveling in from the ocean.

"I am Ganymede, daughter of Europa, greatdaughter of Io of the Warmward Kinship of Great Salmon Eaters."

"I am Phoebe, daughter of Titania."

"I am Mimas, son of Phoebe, greatson of Titania, of the Warmward Kinship."

They have survived another cold season and come home to us. They are not my traveling companions, but they speak my language and we belong to each other. Though I do not see them every season, I feel stronger and braver when we are together.

Aquila and I reach the Gathering Place. Altair hurries to his mother's side and pokes at her belly for milk. He is long past drinking his food but still young enough to ask for comfort milk. A few quick swallows, and he is as cheerful as ever. Deneb peels away from racing with his cousins. He swims around and around me, stroking my sides with his flippers. He rubs his head against the tender places on my chin.

"Sorry," I whisper to him. I nudge him to go back to his cousins, but he sticks by my side, as if to make sure I do not wander off again.

Our kinship holds the long dance each

year in honor of the return of salmon. At first we swim toward each other in long lines. Then the leaping and spinning and splashing begin. Deneb loves this part best and is keen to show all of us how much he has grown. We tell stories of our travels and wild adventures and narrow escapes. I overhear the wayfinders comparing today's sea shake to ones from generations past. I am relieved and proud to hear the old tales. We have endured hard things before. No power of the earth will stop us from gathering.

In all the hubbub, Greatmother comes to Aquila and places a flipper gently on hers. "Well done. You found the way."

Greatmother does not scold me for going off alone. She never scolds. But I feel the sting of what she has not said. I made a mistake. I only thought of how fast I could swim. I only cared about what my mother needed and not what my baby cousin was strong enough to do. Not what was best for my whole family. Wayfinding is a privilege, but it is my birthright too, and I want to be worthy of it. Someday.

CHAPTER FIVE
LONG DANCE

Vega's back! She found us! I knew she would. I turn away from the game with my cousins and swim around and around her. I'm never letting her out of my sight again. We dance our long dance, first in rows of one family swimming toward another, announcing our names as we go. But then comes the fun part: the leaping, the spinning, the racing. I show them all how big and strong I have grown. I roll to one side and the other so that my kinship can remember my fin shadow that gleams like a silver cloud along my back. I try to remember the names and fin shadows and tail shapes of the kin I don't usually travel with.

As the greetings go on past sunset, it's easy to see that Mother and the baby in her belly are the most important ones. There has not been a mother all round-bellied like her in many seasons. It is great luck for the whole kinship when a baby is born. And Mother's is going to be a girl. Even more luck!

"A girl at last!" Aunt Nova says.

"May she be the mother of many someday," Uncle Antares says.

Some of my kin have carried a mouthful of their last meal to share with her. Everyone showers her with loving strokes and soothing click-streams.

Later the gathering settles down. Some of us hunt. Others make a sleep line and doze. I see Vega and Aquila leaving the sleep line to speak with Greatmother. I sneak up on them. I move ever so slowly past the rest of my family. When I am close enough to hear, I close my eye and pretend to sleep.

"One time many hundreds of seasons ago," Greatmother says. "When my greatmother's greatmother was a sleek matriarch in the making like you . . ."

A story! I love stories. I rise for breath along with all the other sleepers, so they won't know I'm listening. Greatmother goes on.

"A tremor came. It was strong like this one. But unlike this one, it did not stop shaking until it remade the shape of the sea and pulled trees and humans and animals from the shore and set them adrift. Dark days followed for all creatures, whether they swam or walked or flew."

My heart is pounding so loud I'm sure it will wake everybody. One click-stream in my direction and they will see I'm not asleep. I squeeze my eye shut.

"Tell me!" Vega and Aquila say together. And Greatmother does tell—stories too horrifying and fantastical to be true. I gulp down every word.

Could it happen again? I wonder, and then, almost as if Greatmother can hear my thoughts, she nuzzles Vega and sighs. "What has happened once is likely to happen again."

"What should we do?" Aquila asks. I move closer so I don't miss a word.

"When the earth shakes, the open ocean is a refuge. But—"

"Mother's baby will come any day now," Vega says. "And the salmon we need to eat are coming here."

"And the currents of the ocean are hard on a newborn," Greatmother adds. "Always remember, together is better than apart."

Yes! I shout it in my own head, even though

it's what I want to bellow in Vega's ear. Together is always better. Uncle Rigel is not wise like the wayfinders, but he says the same.

"So we stay," Vega says, "even though the sea may shake again?"

"We stay today," Greatmother says. "We listen. We learn. And tomorrow we listen again. Learn again. Decide again."

Stay together, I say to myself. *Listen together. Learn together.* I was wrong to doubt my sister. I stop pretending to sleep and move into Vega's swim shadow.

"I will always follow you," I say.

CHAPTER SIX
BIRTH

Mother makes a groan in her sleep and wakes up. Uncle Rigel is beside her, as always. He nudges her skyward to encourage her to breathe.

"Thank you," Mother murmurs.

"It is time," Greatmother announces. She turns to her brother. "Rigel, watch over us."

As if by magic, every wayfinder and great hunter of our kinship wakes and swims to Mother's side.

"I'll help!" I say.

"Mother," Vega says. "Will it be all right? Is it too soon?"

The others shush her and nudge her into

Mother's circle of companions.

"Come with us," Uncle Rigel says to me.

He and Uncle Antares swim on either side of me and turn me away from the circle of care.

"But she needs me." I push against the uncles. How can I leave Mother—and Vega too? I promised I never would. But my uncles are bigger than me and just as determined. They guide me away from the action.

"We will help," Uncle Rigel says.

"We will guard," Uncle Antares adds.

I don't want to guard. I want to be in the circle of companions. But I can't overpower my uncles. They are huge compared to me. Still, I bet I can outsmart them. I point my click-stream at the first rocky crevice I see.

"Oh, look, an octopus!"

Once, when I was quite small, an octopus dared to lay tentacles on me. Uncle Rigel scooped the fellow up by his head and lifted him out of the water in a single leap. He threw the octopus, *splat,* against the side of a passing watcher boat.

Surely the prospect of a lurking octopus will distract my uncles now. I squirm out from between them and head back to the mothers and Vega.

"I'm here!" I announce to the circle of them. "I'll help," I add when my greeting gets no response.

Mother is in the middle. The others are sending comforting pulses of click-stream over her body, from nose to tail.

"Here she comes," Greatmother says in her most soothing voice.

"Almost there," Aunt Nova croons.

A stream of yellow squirts out of Mother's tail end.

"Does it hurt?" Vega says. "Is it awful?"

"Don't be troubled, my bright star," Mother says. "I am strong."

"I'm here!" I call out. "I'll help."

"Hey!" Uncle Antares says, poking me in the belly with his fin. "Come help me chase away sharks."

"I can't leave her!"

"Courage, my sister," Aunt Nova whispers.

"You are strong," says Greatmother Io.

"Strong, strong, strong," Vega and Aquila sing together.

A black and sunrise-pink tail emerges, all curled up amid a cloud of pale yellow water and dark red blood.

"Blood brings sharks," Uncle Antares says, nudging me away from the birth.

"Guard the mothers," Uncle Rigel adds.

It's true, a few blue sharks are streaming toward us. Uncle Rigel is already in the fray, whacking their pointy noses with his broad and sturdy tail. Uncle Antares bites into one and gives it a firm shake before letting go.

Good game! I go after a shark, nipping its tail until it decides to move along. I patrol for more intruders but always circle back to check on Mother.

The last time she had a baby, the baby's tail stayed curled up like a snail in a shell. That baby never had a beating heart. I'm almost afraid to look, but when I do, I see Greatmother gently stroking a tiny and perfectly shaped tail.

Yes! I leap and spin in the air and then roll in the happy fizz of bubbles.

A stray octopus catches my eye—a huge one—walking across the bottom of the sea.

Danger!

I swoop down and take the creature by the head. It immediately wraps three tentacles around me. I spiral in one direction and then spin back the other way, to break its grasp. I give it a firm whack with my tail. It inks me and slithers away. I watch it go with satisfaction and then wave my flippers at the cloud of ink so that it will not drift over and annoy the mothers.

I circle back to them. The wayfinders have moved skyward. They breathe as one. Greatmother and Aunt Nova hold the new baby delicately between them, raising my tiny black and golden-pink sister to the skin of the sea.

Yes! She is born! I leap for joy.

"She's here!" I shout. I spin around the circle of mothers, spiraling with excitement.

No one answers me. Not even Vega.

I stop spiraling. I swim around them, slowly this time. Mother gives a small groan. A thing floats out of her body, as white as a bone and as bendable as a stalk of seagrass. It is baby sized, and empty. It floats for a moment and then sinks into the depths.

"Mother?"

I move closer. No one looks at me. I look at my new sister.

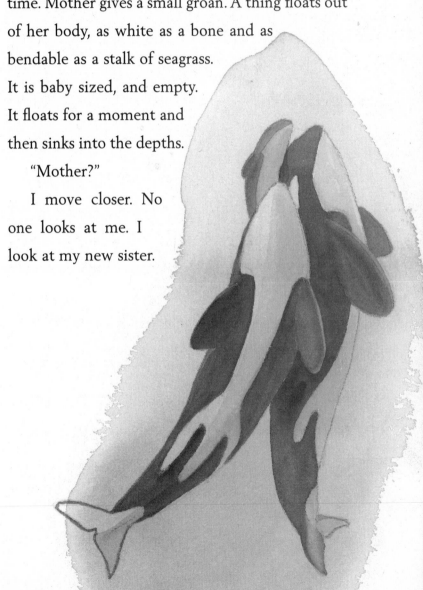

Capella—the one we have all been waiting for, the one who will bring us luck. Aunt Nova lifts her to breathe. Greatmother presses gently against her little stomach. A yellowish stream leaks out of her mouth. Capella's eyes are closed. Her breather on top of her head opens and shuts, but air doesn't go in.

"Mother?" I say again.

A silence falls over the group. Mother faces her baby and click-streams her ever so tenderly.

Is there a heartbeat? I can't tell. I want to reach out to Capella with my own click-stream and see for myself if her breathing parts are filling and emptying as they should, but I don't dare.

Uncle Rigel swims up beside me and faces his sister and all her daughters and greatdaughters. "I am here," he says. "I am beside you."

I long to slip into Uncle Rigel's swim shadow and lean on his strength, as I have so often before. But I'm not my mother's baby. Not anymore. I swim up to Vega and nuzzle her as gently as I can.

"I'm here," I whisper.

Greatmother continues to press Capella's belly as Aunt Nova lifts her to the air. Mother showers Capella with her most gentle clicks, searching for a way to make her breathe.

I can't say how long we wait and watch and hope for Capella to live. I barely notice the thin curve of the moon rising or the stars swimming across the night sky. Rain is falling when Greatmother brings Capella to Mother. She groans and keens in sadness. All the mothers of my kinship add their voices to the lament. It's nothing like any other song they sing—high-pitched and fierce and full of longing.

Their voices bite into my heart and leave me gasping. I want something to fight. Something to fix. Something to sink my teeth into. But there is only sorrow, as cold and mysterious as the depths of the ocean.

CHAPTER SEVEN
STOLEN

The sun rises, and I barely notice.

Capella is gone. Gone like many other babies before her. We are the strongest creatures in all the sea, but this one thing, birth, that comes so easily to others, comes hard for us.

All around me, the mothers of my kinship wail their song of sorrow. Uncle Rigel, faithful as always, swims just beneath Mother, lifting her as he rises for air. No sad whistles from him. Only this. "I am here. I am beside you." Steady as the tide.

I cannot make a sound. My feelings are stuck like ice inside me. Capella was going to be my sister, my forever companion. She was the one I would travel with all my life. Aquila will go back to Aunt Nova and travel with her someday. Capella was the one I was going to share everything with: the wayfinding and the hunt, the lean times and the feast, the endless things I have to learn and the lonely decisions I will have to make, and the quiet beauty of the smallest everyday things. How will I do it all—or any of it—without her?

Greatmother makes a long and careful explanation. ". . . Not our fault . . . the sea has changed . . . poisons flow into the water. . . ."

I am too sad for words to reach me. I drift, feeling nothing.

When the last star has faded away, Greatmother says, "It is over. We must let her go."

Then like the sudden jolt of the earth, my anger breaks free. I cannot. I will not let my sister sink. Not here. Not alone in a dark, cold passage where boats of all kinds will go roaring over her body. Never! I do what, before this moment, I could not have imagined.

I spin away from the circle of grief and swim directly at my mother. I close my eyes, grit my teeth, and crash headlong into her, breaking Capella away from her place on Mother's back. I swoop over my mother and under my sister, lifting her lifeless body onto my own back. I carry her away. I close my heart to the cries of my family.

Aunt Nova's outrage: "You have no right!"

Aquila's pleading: "I will be a sister to you. I promise. I promise."

Deneb calling her name.

Mother's wordless wail of grief.

And under them all, Uncle Rigel's steady voice. "I am here. I am beside you."

I turn away, gather my cold resolve, and spend my strength on speed. I race along the edge of the island in a blind rage. I power past one bay and inlet after another. I dodge spires of rocks. The smooth amber trunks of kelp whoosh along my sides as I go. Seals swerve out of my path. The island narrows to a point.

I pause and draw in a shuddering breath. There

is a solid rocky bank beneath me. It is not dark and cold. Light could reach Capella here, and the music of the rain and wind. I could let her go. I should. But I will not. Her body is still warm against my skin. She is soft and tender and the sea is full of teeth.

I keep swimming. Capella rides my back, curved around my top fin and held in place by the press of water. Capella's body is smooth and sleek, perfect in every way, except for breath. As I carry her, depths yawn open beneath us. I dodge around seamounts with no thought of eating or even of finding my way home.

The sun is at the top of the sky when I find myself face-to-face with the most dangerous passage in the Salish Sea. Deception Pass, we have called it, ever since the last capture and the stealing of Mother's youngest sister,

Andromeda, and many of her cousins.

I did not mean to come here. Did not plan to arrive at the precise moment when Push gives way to Pull and the waters pause as a living creature does between one breath and the next. It is the perfect time to risk this swiftest of all passages. Deception Pass is not long, but it flows between towering walls of rock. A thin spire of an island stands between the walls. A bridge spans from cliff to spire to opposite cliff far, far above. Other sharp spires stand under the water. Only the heartiest creatures can live where the current is so strong.

But now the waters lie still before me. I feel calm, and a flash of certainty comes over me. It is right that I am here with my sister. Right that I tell Capella the story of our mother's courage and the mighty deeds of Uncle Rigel and his brothers. Most of all, it feels right that she should rest in honor alongside the heroes of our kinship.

I take a deep breath and move carefully through the neck of the passage.

"A great battle was fought here," I tell my sister. "Back in the rough days when our mother was a bitty thing, nearly as small as you. Back when humans in net boats fired their metal teeth into our sides. Back when younglings were stolen from the sea and carried away."

I swim into the calm of the bay beyond Deception Pass, telling the story as it was once told to me.

"A generation ago, when Greatmother and Uncle Rigel were young and Mother was a tiny thing like you, the capture boats hunted them. Three boats followed our family that day. And a giant thundering creature flew above them. They chased them up one passage and down another.

"Finally Greatmother made a desperate plan. She brought her family here to this passage, which we called the Narrow at the time. She knew it was the young the humans wanted, so she split her family up at the opening of the Narrow. Greatmother led the larger group. Her brothers took a smaller group and all of the babies and younglings with them. They dove deep and turned in to the Narrow. They held their breath to the point of bursting, swam past the stone spires and into the bay. They turned warmward, where the humans would not see them.

"It worked. All three boats followed Greatmother coldward. Uncle Rigel and his brothers gathered the little ones together and held them close, keeping silence. But then the flying creature found them and the chaser boats followed it, small boats, but fast and carrying nets. The babies were already weary when the net dropped.

Uncle Rigel and his brothers fought with all their strength. The humans in the boats fought back with metal claws and ropes. The battle raged until sundown, and the waters of the cove ran red with our blood.

"Uncle Rigel broke a hole in the net, and with the help of his brothers he took Aunt Nova to freedom. He went back for Mother. He was slashed with a boat hook, but he did not give up. He guided Mother to safety while the humans wrestled Andromeda and her cousins into slings and lifted them out of the water. They were never heard nor seen again, in all the length of the Salish Sea or even the ocean beyond. Uncle Rigel's brothers died that day, and their bodies rest on the sandy bottom of the place we call Blood Cove. Mother and Aunt Nova were the only babies to survive."

I pause. Close my eyes. Let go a heavy *chaaaah* of breath. It has been many seasons since I came here with Greatmother, but I remember the shape of this shore. My destination lies ahead. I go slower now, and Capella feels heavier. The weight of all the time we will never have drags me down. A sister is a life bond. We could have spent four hundred seasons together. I will feel this pain with the turn of every season. But today I will be brave. For her.

"I'm taking you there, little Capella," I say. "To Blood Cove. I will lay you beside the bones of the uncles who saved your mother. You will not be alone."

I travel slowly, carefully. I rock Capella gently and sing to her. It is not wrong, cannot be wrong, to take my sister to this place and tell her this story. It is her birthright and she *had* lived; her heart *was* beating, if only for a moment.

CHAPTER EIGHT
BLOOD COVE

When Greatmother first told me of the Blood Cove captures, I did not sleep for days. I hunted up and down the islands for humans in the little dragonfly boats, secretly hoping to overturn one and steal their young.

Mother and Greatmother kept to my side in those angry days. They did not scold me. They showed me their own

anger. Together we thrashed our bodies against the skin of the sea. We tore apart giant kelps and shouted the names of our stolen family.

I imagined how it would feel to break a dragonfly boat apart. I planned how I would seize the littlest human in my teeth and hold it, breather down, in the water. I thought about how I would shake that human and beat it against the rocks until the middle bone broke and it could never move again.

I chose the cave where I would take it and leave it to be devoured by all the eyeless toothy things that lurk on the bottom of the sea. I dreamed of a day when the cave would be full of bones.

We went to the shore where humans came to watch us travel, where they sit on hillsides and perch on the rocks in reach of the water.

"Do they know that I could take them?" I said.

"Difficult to say what a human knows," Mother answered.

"They know how to hunt us," I said.

I did not care how long ago the captures were. It felt like they had just happened. I swam up and down in front of the watchers as they waved and shouted at me. I could have taken one. Easy.

Greatmother swam right beside me; her flipper brushed my skin. Her steady breathing reminded me to breathe.

"They are small," Greatmother said.

True. Humans have hardly a scrap of muscle or fat on them. No wonder they cannot swim or fly.

A group of humans standing together caught my eye. Two were small and three were tiny. I swam right up to them. A bigger human held the tiny ones by their grabbers. The smallest one of all was lifted into the spindly flippers of the largest one, almost as if they were taking care of it. They chirped softly to each other.

"They do not have families," I said to Greatmother. "How could they when they are so cruel?"

One of the tiny humans pointed a grabber at me. It cooed like a bird. The other flapped and squeaked. The bigger human held them tight. I looked right at them and they looked right at me.

"The wayfinders do not agree about whether humans make families," Greatmother said. "What do you think?"

I went out to deeper water and thought for a long time. When I came back to the rocks, some of the humans had gone, but the group by the water was still there, the same five. They still chattered to each other. They were feeding. The bigger human gave something tan and flat to the tiny one. It broke the flat thing in two pieces and gave a piece to the other tiny human. They put the thing in their mouths, even though it was not wet or shiny or fat or wiggling. Clearly these humans knew nothing about good things to eat. No wonder they were so small.

But they shared. Even though they only had a little food, they shared just like us.

I swam away that evening. Still angry. Still sad. But not so hungry for revenge.

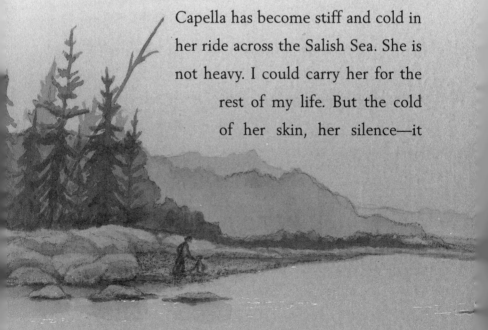

Capella has become stiff and cold in her ride across the Salish Sea. She is not heavy. I could carry her for the rest of my life. But the cold of her skin, her silence—it would break me. We enter Blood Cove. The bones of the heroes lie below us. I should let Capella go. This is what I have come to do. And yet my heart does not ache any less.

Along the water's edge I spy a human walking side by side with a smaller human. They hold grabbers as they walk. The Pull grows stronger. Clams retreat into the sand and muck. Barnacles draw their feathery tongues back into their shells, and anemones close up the flower of their tentacles. A strip of rocks and sand is laid bare by the retreating water, and the littler human kneels down to pick up shells and scoop sand.

The bigger human sees me, but unlike most humans, she does not wave or shout. She does not point me out to the littler human, who must be her own youngling. She walks slowly, her hair blowing like kelp fronds about her. She cradles her long and spindly flippers around a great bulge in her middle. Humans come in many sizes, and in all the colors from palest sand to deepest night. But I have never seen, up close, a human with this middle bulge before. I linger at the surface and watch.

The human hums. I have always assumed that humans were egg-laying creatures like the birds who go ashore to have their babies. But this human clearly has an inward egg. She stops. Looks at me. Looks at me and my sister. She places a flipper over her throat. She walks slowly into the water, stopping only when the water reaches her middle bulge. Humans do not travel in the sea without a boat. They have not nearly enough fat and cannot

bear the cold. But this human is bearing the cold.

Only a few body lengths of water lie between us. Water and sorrow. I know the sea is changing. I can taste the poisons. I know they are hard for a baby to bear. But are the poisons bad for all babies? Do they harm even human babies? Maybe not. The poisons leak out of human things and run off human places. And there are many more humans than orcas. Still, I wonder.

"What touches the water touches us all," Mother always says when something perplexing happens. "Watch the water. Always. Do not look away from what you do not understand. Sometimes it will happen in a heartbeat and sometimes in a hundred seasons, but whatever touches the water will touch us all."

Uncle Rigel is not so chatty and not so wise. He only says, "I am beside you; I will help."

To my surprise, it is Uncle Rigel's words that set my course now. Perhaps there is nothing more than to swim beside those you love and help them with all your strength. I should go to my family and bear my fears as best I can. At least I will not be alone.

So in the end I say nothing, and perhaps the human understands nothing. We spend a few heartbeats of our long lives looking at each other across the water. And then we turn away, not quite the same creatures we had been before. I go to the bones of the heroes and place my sister gently among them, their tall ribs forming a guard to stand around her for all time.

CHAPTER NINE
FOLLOW

I watch my sister swim away with Capella's body. I should stop her. I should bring Capella back. I'm their only brother. But I'm my mother's only son. I should stay with her and stand watch. Thinking of all the things I should do squeezes the air right out of me. I lift my head into the dreary fog of morning, gasping.

My uncles swim beneath Mother and Greatmother, nudging them skyward to breathe. Uncle Rigel, the oldest of them all, swims apart from the rest, nose pointing in the direction Vega has gone. He sends out his most powerful click-stream. He calls her name. He looks above the water, and then drops below to call again. He listens.

I watch him and do the same.

No answering call comes back. How could she do this? Run off—again! How could she do it now? I take my place beside Uncle Rigel. We see fish large and little, squids and crabs, net boats and wind boats, and soaring eagles. But not Vega.

"Where did she go?" I whisper.

"Warmward. Along this shore," Uncle Rigel

says. "Jump. See if you can spot her from the air."

I've never felt less like jumping. Still, when it's loud, sometimes you can see things above the water that are hidden by all the noise below. I circle downward and then point to the sky. I pump my flukes with all my strength and burst into the air, high enough to clear the water. I search for the black swoop of Vega's fin. I jump again.

Nothing.

Vega is always the one keeping me from

wandering off after some interesting fish or curious boat. It feels wrong for her to be gone, like having a flipper stripped away. I turn to my uncle.

"I should go and get her. I should bring her back."

"She must come home," Uncle Rigel says. "We need her now more than ever. But hear me well, Deneb. Wayfinders will never follow their brothers. They will go where their hearts and their memories tell them to go."

My flukes droop at the corners. What if she doesn't want to come home? Maybe she wants Capella more than me.

Uncle Rigel thrums thoughtfully.

"Even so, you must try. A wayfinder needs a brother at her side." Uncle Rigel stretches his broad flipper toward mine. "You must help her to see the way clearly," he says. "Your trust will make her strong. Your steadfastness will help her chose the right path."

"What if I can't even find her?"

I am bigger than I was last season, and much

bigger than the season before. But the sea is as huge as the sky.

"You have followed your sister all your life. You know her. It is your heart that will find her in the end—though all your thoughts and all your strength will be needed too."

I can still hear the circle of mothers, singing their haunting song of goodbye.

"Vega will lead you back to us," Uncle Rigel says firmly. "Trust her. She is wiser than she knows."

I take a breath and another. Does he really want me to leave? To swim away? I have only ever followed.

"Finding is not leaving," Uncle Rigel says. "Finding her is a kind of following. Go as far as the end of this island and no more. If Vega is not there, my voice will guide you back."

I look toward the mothers all tangled together in sorrow. I nuzzle Uncle Rigel once. I let out the boldest *chaaaah* of breath that I can make, and then swim away.

I fight the morning Push. It's harder with no one to swim alongside and shelter me. I swing my head from side to side, click-streaming the steep sides of the island. Spindly seaweeds and strange-looking creatures live at the bottom of these underwater cliffs. Vega is not here.

I remember the shallow plain by the blinking light, where there are no trees on the shore. It's always bright there. I head that way, swimming faster now. Suddenly certain, as Uncle Rigel said I would be, that Vega is looking for a place to leave Capella's body. Not a dark place. No, she will leave her in the sunlight.

The fog lifts and the sun is well above the mountains when I reach the warmward tip of the island.

"Vega!" I shout. "Vega?" I send out clicks as loud as I can, to search for the shape of her.

Seals are everywhere I look. They nose along the rocky bottom and snap up the spiky little fish they like to eat. They swirl away from me as I swim by. Ordinarily I would play tag with them, but I can't abandon my quest. I circle back and search again. Vega is nowhere to be found. I was sure she'd be here!

I can barely hear Uncle Rigel now. If I go on without his voice to guide me, I might never find

the way home. The dread of being alone presses in on me like deep water. I gather my courage. Vega needs me. Ahead is another passage and then another island, and more after that. I will search them all.

The sun is at the top of the sky, and I've looked into every inlet. I've found more things than I can even name: slugs of every color and shape, the sea star with the skinny points, the swimming bird with the black beak and red triangles, the wading bird with the red beak and black triangles. But no Vega. Not a hint of her. No matter how many times I call, she doesn't answer.

I rest for a moment at the broad passage that leads to the territory of the Coldward Kinship of Salmon Eaters. They aren't enemies, not exactly. But the Coldward ways are strange, and nobody understands them when they speak.

Would Vega go that way? Would she leave her home waters? Warmward would take her to more familiar places. But there's more boat noise in the warmward end of the sea. I wait for my heart to tell me where she is, as Uncle Rigel promised it would.

One thing is certain. She would never go straight ahead through Deception Pass. Not ever. Dark stories are told of that path. Mother has never said exactly what happened there, but I've overheard stories of the capture seasons and the stolen younglings. Sometimes when Mother sleeps, her whole body shivers and she groans.

Greatmother always nudges her awake, saying, "It is over now. It is done."

Mother goes to Uncle Rigel when she has the nightmares and rubs her chin gently over the long scar that runs from his flipper up across his back to the base of his fin. He is the bravest of us all.

"Thank you," she whispers to him. "Thank you."

Sometimes when she and Greatmother think everyone is asleep, they circle down to

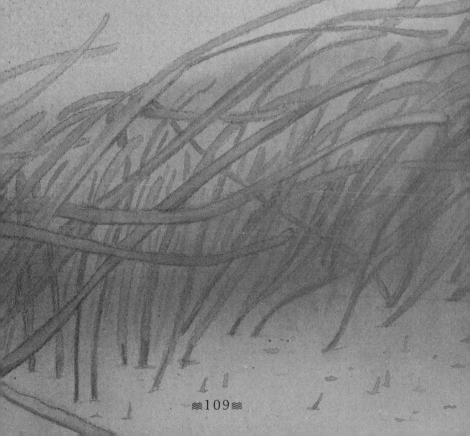

the depths where their voices will carry a long way and call for Andromeda and all the stolen younglings. Sometimes, when no one is listening, I call their names too, so that their memory will not be lost forever.

Vega would never go to such a sad place. She'd look for a peaceful place. A place with good memories. I imagine Vega swimming ahead of me. I think of her going to someplace safe and beautiful.

Coldward, I decide. There is an island nearby with all trees and no humans. Tree Island is where she first taught me to catch salmon when I was no bigger than Altair. The memory of it makes me happy. Uncle Rigel is right. My heart will show me the way. I swim through the broad passage, on the right path at last.

CHAPTER TEN
RESCUE

I head for Tree Island, calling Vega's name as I go. I'm sure I'll find her where she first taught me to hunt—my favorite place. Net boats are out, but I dodge them. I duck into a bay to let a thing carrier roar by. In the quiet after the thing carrier passes, I hear the high-pitched squeaks of porpoises hunting squid.

This passage is not as deep as the one where my kinship gathers. I can easily swim to the bottom. I can tell I have come to the right island by the many pillars of rock around its edge. I call Vega's name. I circle the island.

Vega's not here. I was so sure she would be. I think over my plan again. I look above the water and then below. The trunks of the kelp forest shift in the Pull, and I spy an orca shape hiding.

"Vega!" I trill out the sharpest whistle I can make. "VEGA!"

She doesn't answer. I move closer still.

"Vega?"

She looks too big, but it's hard to tell because of the waving trunks of kelp. I rise to the surface for a better look. Vega rises too, and in a flash I see my mistake. A tall fin breaks the skin of the sea and a great huff of breath makes an upward cloud that could only come from a male orca as big as Uncle Rigel. His fin shape is wrong, and the gray fin shadow on his back is not one I've seen before. This orca is from the Seal-eating Kinship—a stranger to me. I back away, looking for the stranger's family, so that I can keep a respectful distance.

I blast out my click-stream in all directions, but no other orca is near. And this big orca is behaving very oddly. Something is caught on his flukes. A line. The end of the line disappears in the rocks. It's only long enough to let him breathe. He can't follow his mother or his sisters. He's all alone.

"Hello," I call out, trying to sound bigger than I am. "I am Deneb, son of Arctura, of the Warmward Salmon Eaters."

The big male says nothing at all.

I make a sprint around Tree Island again. Still no Vega. I come face-to-face with the big male. My heart races, not because I'm afraid; I'm never afraid! But being stuck, being held still while the whole sea moves around you, that seems like the worst thing that could happen to anyone. I should keep looking for Vega, but I don't want to leave him trapped.

"Hello," I say again.

The big orca makes an odd-sounding grunt that could mean anything at all.

I click-stream carefully down the line. It connects to a cage on the bottom with a few crabs in it.

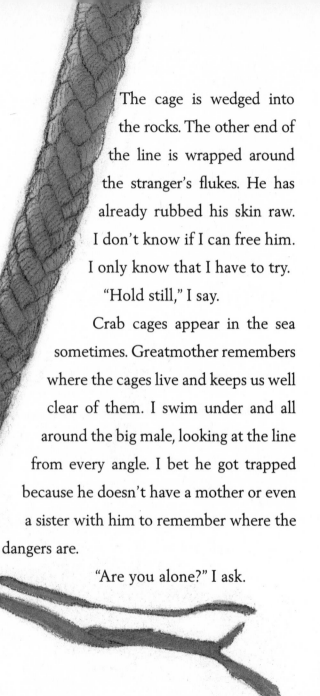

The cage is wedged into the rocks. The other end of the line is wrapped around the stranger's flukes. He has already rubbed his skin raw. I don't know if I can free him. I only know that I have to try.

"Hold still," I say.

Crab cages appear in the sea sometimes. Greatmother remembers where the cages live and keeps us well clear of them. I swim under and all around the big male, looking at the line from every angle. I bet he got trapped because he doesn't have a mother or even a sister with him to remember where the dangers are.

"Are you alone?" I ask.

The stranger answers with two grunts and a mysterious crackling noise. The Seal-eating Kinship are not the chatty types. The stranger rises to the surface and draws in a weary breath.

"Have you seen another orca all alone today? Carrying a tiny baby?"

The stranger only groans and tugs at the line.

"I didn't think so," I mumble.

Greatmother has told me to keep clear of the Seal-eaters, but I don't care. I can't just swim away. I don't know what will happen if I set him free. Will he hurt me? Sometimes the Seal-eaters eat the babies of scooper and gulper whales. I am only a little bit bigger than a baby whale.

No, I tell myself firmly. *Orcas don't eat other orcas.* There are rules. Still, I keep clear of the biting end.

"I'm here to help you," I say.

If I can lift the trap up, maybe I can work the line free. Two crabs inside the trap wave their claws at each other and snatch bites from a chunk of fish.

I'm not putting my mouth or my tongue anywhere near those pinchers. Still, I can't see another way. Maybe a stick will help. I like sticks. Things change when you poke them. Anemones close up. Clams dig deeper into the sand. Octopuses ink.

"Be right back," I say.

I am halfway around the island when I hear the high-pitched buzz of a little boat. I peek above the water and see an orange watcher boat with two humans speeding straight toward the big orca. The orange boat does not stop three leaps away and just watch, like other watcher boats do. They must be up to something.

I've heard some things about the captures. Uncle Rigel boldly rescued Mother and Aunt Nova—he alone of his brothers survived. The dashing scar he wears on his back is our reminder of that day. He never speaks of the rescues. But I imagine what happened all the time. The battle, the danger, and the glory at the end.

I could be a rescuer. I have fought my way

bravely through great patches of sinister eelgrass and rescued drift logs from the clutches of a rocky cove. I have once—twice now—tangled with a great octopus and lived to tell the tale. And here is my chance. A capture! Right in front of me! I lurk underneath the boat and plot the grand rescue.

"Harm not the humans," Greatmother has told me more than once. "No matter what they do, never touch them."

I don't know how I'm going to save the stranger orca without touching the humans; it's a heroic puzzle. I see the shadow of a long and narrow flipper reaching toward the tangled orca. He edges away, but the line holds him fast.

A great splash, I decide. Everyone knows that humans hate water. They shriek like gulls whenever they are splashed. Even when you see them jump into the water on purpose, they yelp and thrash about in a frenzy like a hermit crab all out of its shell. Yes, a mighty splash. Nothing else will do.

I circle out to deeper water, turn, and then head

for the orange boat at top speed. I aim my jump to come just before the boat. I arch my back, give one last push, and burst out of the water. I crash down and a great whoosh of water goes over the boat. I pop up again to watch the humans surrender.

They don't retreat. The human reaches toward the stranger again, a sharp claw in its grabbers. Capturers for sure! And after all these years!

"I'll save you," I call.

I gulp in water, lift my head in the air, and balance my flippers flat on the surface. The human is holding the line in one flipper and is sawing away at it with the claw. I take aim, and spit a stream of water right in the human's face.

It shouts, shakes water from its head and flippers, and goes straight back to menacing the stranger. The monster!

"Don't panic!" I call to the stranger, who is clearly frozen with fear and letting the human touch him without punishment. "I won't give up! I promise."

If only I had a good stick or a big octopus to

throw! Even a medium-sized octopus would do the trick. I swim beneath the orange boat again. I can hear the sound of the claw at work above. It's now or never. I aim for the edge of the orange boat and swim straight up. The boat is soft, like a jelly. I tilt it up into the air. Both humans squawk like ravens. Objects clatter and fall into the water. The human with the claw follows.

Unlike other humans, no thrashing. It holds on to the line and gives a great jab with its claw. My heart is pounding.

"Stop!" I shout. "He isn't hurting you! None of us ever hurt you!" I squirt a furious blast of bubbles underneath the human.

And then, just like that, the human listens! The line uncoils from the stranger's flipper and falls away, leaving a ring of raw skin behind. The human takes its claw and climbs back into the boat. The humans turn around, fire up the growler . . . and before I can chase them, they speed away. It's incredible!

"I did it! I saved you!" I swim in circles, slapping

my tail on the skin of the sea and letting the boom of it echo through the water. "I did it! I did it!"

The stranger swirls through the water, leaping in the air with relief and gratitude. He circles back to me. Makes a single long whistle and then swims off.

The Seal-eating families are a peculiar bunch— everyone says so. Still, I'm sad to see him go. It's lonely to travel all by myself, to come to a crossing of currents and not have a mother or sister to choose the way. The sea is bigger and more wild than I ever imagined. I'm afraid if I keep going coldward, away from Mother and Greatmother, I'll never find them again. Vega wouldn't go this far. Would she? No. I have missed her somehow. I'll turn back and keep searching.

CHAPTER ELEVEN
LONGBOATS

Though I have let my sister go, my body is heavy as I swim out of Blood Cove. Leaving Capella behind is like ripping out a hook. I will never be the same. I want my mother. Want her like I did when I was a tiny youngling.

I head back to Deception Pass. It is easier to swim without Capella, but it feels wrong to swim alone. Not frightening, not exactly. The only creatures in the sea bigger than me do not have teeth. Still,

it is unnerving
to breathe without
my family rising beside me.
A few swift boats zip by, the kind that
have lines with a hook on the end to kill fish. I
swerve to stay clear of them. I zigzag. I dive. It
is exhausting. I wish it was night and the boats
would all go away. But then I hear another sound,

a gentler sound. I stop
and call on my memories.

Could it be true? Are the longboat
riders in the water today? I listen again for the
splash and the swirling, so much like the sound a
swimming bird makes. Each longboat has a beak
on the front, like a raven. I pop up for a look.
And there they are, the longboat riders—many of

them. They travel in a line, like geese in the sky. They gather every salmon season, just like my own kinship.

The old stories tell of a time when all the boats in the Salish Sea were as quiet as these. In those days, boats did not bleed poison. No one tried to capture orcas. And the salmon ran so thick and strong that not a single orca of any kinship ever knew hunger. There were so many fish that rivers shone silver in the summer sun.

Greatmother has stories from when she was a youngling. "The longboat riders were the defenders of clams," she said. "They built shelters for them along the shore, and traps for salmon. We had a settled way between us. They hunted the salmon in the rivers and coves, and we hunted them in the sea."

Why couldn't I have been born then, when the sea was quieter and all its water tasted clean? When I would have had many sisters?

I swim near the longboats. Two of them are about as big as me, and one is bigger. Many humans ride them, dipping their narrow wings into the water together as though they are one creature.

Greatmother always greets them as kin, so I call out my name.

"I am Vega, daughter of Arctura, greatdaughter of Siria of the Warmward Kinship of Salmon Eaters."

They call back to me. Not shouting or clicking lights—only gentle sounds and an outstretched wing. I travel alongside them, like they are family, until they turn and go ashore at the mouth of a river.

I swim into the entrance to Deception Pass. The Pull is in full force. I can hear the rush of water through the narrow channel. A tall and steep-sided island stands in the pass at its narrowest point. The force of the water tugs me forward, but I linger in the lea of the island to look ahead. Not a boat is in sight to fight the pull of the narrows, but I hear the faint drone of land boats on the bridge far above. In the distance I catch the shape of an orca. A big one. Uncle Rigel! I click-stream again. The outline of a smaller orca following the larger one bounces back to me.

"Deneb!" I shout. "Uncle Rigel!"

Who else could it be?

"I'm here! I'm coming home!"

A great longing for the sight and touch and sound of my family wells up in me. I have never, in my whole life, been away from them for so long. I rush forward as fast as I can go.

I am in the narrowest part of the pass when a great *BOOM* resounds all around me, so loud the very force of the sound pushes me upward. The bottom of the sea jolts forward and back.

BOOM! POP! CRASH!

Stone grinds against stone. The whole sea goes dark from the noise. It presses against my body as if I am in water so deep no light can reach me.

"Uncle Rigel!" I shout. "Deneb!"

CRASH! BOOM! BANG! rolls up from the depths.

My ears throb. The island sways. The bridge above crackles. A land boat and a chunk of the bridge tumble into the water, blocking one side of the passage.

I gasp in panic. Draw in the biggest breath my body can hold and plunge onward. My belly grazes the bottom of the sea.

CHAPTER TWELVE
SEA SHAKE

The first jolt hits me like thunder.

BOOM! POP! CRACK!

Everything goes fuzzy.

CRASH! WHAM!

The bottom of the sea jerks back and forth. Huge boulders splash down from cliff tops.

The stranger calls out to me in the chaos. "Deep!" he shouts, plain as day. "Go deep!" he calls again. Then he turns to the passage that leads to the ocean and swims away at top speed.

I race to the stranger's side. I don't know if his

swim shadow will protect me. I hope so. I fight with all my strength to keep up.

The sand and stone of the sea floor is a blur of motion. We swim above the rising murk of silty water. Fish hang stunned, not moving at all. But the stranger and I charge forward.

A swarm of porpoises surges past us. They pour on speed, leaping into the air to escape the pressure of sound.

"Deep!" they chirp as they pass. "Deep! Deep!"

I've never understood porpoises before. Like them, I leap through the air to escape the grinding noise of stone on stone.

I see Deception Pass. The hills on either side of the pass are blurry with motion. Land boats fall from the bridge, and a section breaks away and plunges into the water.

"Vega!" I shout as I splash back into the roiling sea.

How will I ever find her now?

CHAPTER THIRTEEN
DECEPTION PASS

I cannot believe what I am seeing. Another piece of the bridge tumbles into the water, and land boats fall after it. The wake from the splash rolls me end over end. I struggle to right myself. I think I hear someone calling my name in all the jumble of noise.

"Deneb!" I scream. It must be my brother. Who else is foolish enough to follow me?

Clouds of sand rise from the groaning sea floor. Ahead I see a family of porpoises, leaping one after another and heading toward the ocean.

"Go deep," Greatmother had said. "When the sea shakes, the open ocean is a refuge."

"Deneb!" I scream again. I cannot leave him behind. How will he know which way to go? I leap as high as I can and look across the water. Where is he? Did I imagine his voice?

No. Deneb will be with Uncle Rigel, and he will be with Mother and Greatmother, and they will be leading the whole family to the safety of the open ocean. All I have to do is catch up. The sea churns with the power of a hundred winter storms. I turn toward the ocean and swim with all my strength, noise-blind but navigating by memory. I will find my family.

CHAPTER FOURTEEN
WAVES

The shaking stops just as I clear Deception Pass. The press of sound falls away. I stop too. Take a breath, a breath, and another breath. The silence that follows the shaking is almost as scary as the noise. I send a click-stream out through the churned-up water to get my bearings. The ocean lies straight ahead, a full day's journey away.

A scooper whale and her baby charge past me. I did not know they could go so fast.

The scooper whale chants, "Deep, deep." An Orca word, clear as sunlight. They head for the ocean. Fish hang dazed in the water, not moving at all.

"Deneb!" I call. "Mother!"

What have I done? Gone off and left my family. Again! I was sure I could retrace my path. Sure they would wait for me. What if I never find them?

Another whale swoops past. A singing whale. He calls out, "Deep, deep." In Orca. Just like the scooper.

I follow the singing whale. Usually they are such dawdlers. Lazily circling clumps of fish. Lunging through them, mouths agape. But this one has closed his mouth tight and tucked his long flippers close to his body. He pumps his gigantic tail and pulls me along in his wake. Stray crab cages bounce off his sides and swirl away from him. I see dim shapes in the water: porpoises, a scooper whale and her baby . . . or is it Deneb? Could that be Aquila and little Altair? I shout their names, but all I hear back from every creature of the sea who can speak is, "Deep, deep, go deep."

The Pull feels stronger than before. A new

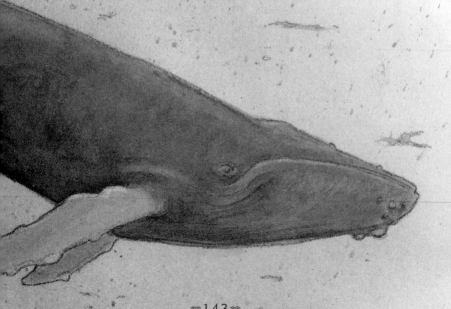

sound comes from the bottom of the sea. A clatter, not like the breaking of solid rock, but like the rolling of stones. The singing whale swerves to avoid a net boat.

As we swim past, the net breaks free, spilling its catch of salmon. I snatch one and gulp it down. The net boat turns to the open ocean at top noise.

The sound of rolling stones grows, and the tug of the Pull grows with it. I have never felt a Pull so strong. Not in all my life, not in the worst storms of winter. Swept up in this Pull, I am going faster than I ever have before. When I surface for air, I look around, amazed to see that I am more than halfway to the ocean.

The drumbeat chant, "Deep, deep," strikes me from all sides. I stop looking for my family. I know only that the call belongs to those who share something with my family, something wise, but long buried. A will to survive. But not just will—any little crab or jelly has the same. Will, and the knowledge to navigate by. However different the other whales might be, they are my family in this. I chant along with them, "Deep, deep," as we all strive to reach the open ocean.

And then in the jumble of noise I hear a familiar voice, chanting just like me.

"Deneb!" I shout.

I send a click-stream, narrow and strong, in the direction of the voice. An image comes back—a brother-sized orca, and a big one. Uncle Rigel! I turn crosswise to the current and fight to reach them. The Pull takes hold of me like a howling wind, the kind that turns boats upside down. I grit my teeth and swim with all my might.

"Deneb!" I call.

"Vega!" Deneb yells back. "I found you!"

I close the distance between us and slip into Uncle Rigel's swim shadow. I murmur my thanks, and we keep moving. Something is coming for us. I feel it, like the memory of a nightmare. One menace chasing us out to the ocean, and another charging toward us from the very place of our safety. But how can that be true? Greatmother said, "Deep water is a refuge." She would not lie. Could she be mistaken?

"Uncle Rigel!" I call. "How far must we go?"

He does not answer.

"Rigel!"

I glance at him. There is a notch along the edge of his fluke that I never saw before.

"Uncle?"

"Don't worry," Deneb says. "He's my . . . my . . . not-cousin."

"Not-cousin?"

"I like him."

There is no word for an orca you like who is not in your kinship. I take a closer look. His fin shape is a little bit off, and he sounds funny too. He must be a seal eater. How did this happen?

"Deneb, he's a stranger. Where is Uncle Rigel? Where is *Mother?*"

"I saved him from a tangle, and he helped me find you."

"You what? Where is our family?"

Did Deneb leave them too? Did he follow me? He would never. He is too little. A jolt of panic zings through me. I want my mother, like an ache in my bones, like hunger.

"How deep is enough?" Deneb asks.

I do not know. I only feel danger coming. I leap to look for the way. A line of boats charges toward the ocean. I can see the place ahead where the land stops and the ocean begins. Almost there! I leap again. On the horizon, a wave rises.

The stranger orca must feel it coming too. He stops swimming. He turns to Deneb, fixes him with a firm gaze, and grunts something neither of us understands. He floats near the surface, breathing in and out deeply. I do the same, and Deneb copies me. The air warms me through and gives my tired muscles new strength. I check the horizon again. The wave is taller than boats, taller than trees, tall like the rocky cliffs at Land's End. Panic gives way to dread. Greatmother's voice rings in my memory, "A great tremor came that did not stop shaking until it remade the shape of the sea."

This is a wave to remake the shape of the sea. This is a wave to crush mountains. I scream my mother's name in the face of the giant wave. I left my family, and this is my fate: to face the reshaping of the sea without them.

"I'm right here," Deneb squeaks. "I'm beside you."

I reach for him in the swirling pull of water until he is in the shelter of my flippers. The stranger ducks his head and lifts his tail for a dive.

"Dive!" I shout. "Stay with me!"

The wave is almost upon us. Boats climb up the face of it and tumble backward.

"Ready!" I take a deep breath. "Go!"

I dive, Deneb beside me and the stranger just ahead. The light fades from pale green to deepest blue. I feel the wave draw near. The bottom is flat

here, with no pillars to hide behind. I fight the great wave with all my strength. My heart slows to save breath. Deneb starts to rise, despite the pumping of his little flukes. I move above him and tilt him downward, using my weight to keep him from being swept away. We reach the gravelly bottom. My heart beats slower and slower, even as the wave moves relentlessly toward our home waters.

When it finally passes, we turn skyward and break through the skin of the sea with a great burst of outgoing breath. The stranger makes a loud *chaaaah!* when he surfaces beside us. I draw in courage with each new breath but lose it a little as I look around. Overturned boats and things and humans bob in the water. Some float.

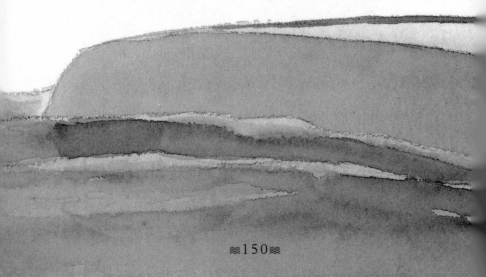

Some sink. Some thrash and shout.

"Oh," Deneb gasps. "Broken."

He goes to the nearest thrashing human and nudges it toward a floating thing. It climbs on, and Deneb goes after the next one. He nudges and lifts until two humans are lying on top of the floating thing. The humans have no proper fat on them. They cling to each other and shiver.

"We have to go," I say.

I look around for the fins of my family, for someone else to take the lead and make the choices. But we are alone.

The overturned boats make me nervous. A fish has gooey bits in the middle that are quite tasty, but a boat has poison at the middle. Soon it will

be oozing into the sea. Still, Greatmother has rules about not hurting humans. Letting them sink is a hurt. But letting Deneb suffer poison is wrong too.

"Just one more," Deneb says, circling back for the last of them. This one bobs at the surface with a floater and a flashing light.

"We have to go *now*!"

I help him nudge the human toward rescue. The others pull it from the water. They clasp each other tight and roar like beached sea lions.

"More giant waves will come," I tell Deneb. "Greatmother told me they travel together, just as we do." Already I am looking for the next one. "We

need deeper water." The stranger is already heading that way.

We turn our backs to the Salish Sea and follow the stranger to Land's End. We wait beside the offshore island, looking and longing for our family to find us. As the sun falls into the sea and the stars rise, so giant waves rise out of the deep. Three of these giants pass over us. Three times we dive. The waves try to pick us up and throw us against the side of the cliffs. We fight them. We hear the sound of the waves hurling their might against the shore. It fades as we are pulled farther and farther away. I close my heart and my memory to my home waters. It is too much. I will never go back.

CHAPTER FIFTEEN
LAND'S END

The ocean is still by the time the sun rises. A night of fighting the giant waves has dragged us away from Land's End to the very edge of the sheer underwater drop that marks the beginning of the open ocean. No light can reach the base of this cliff. No orca knows the creatures who dwell in the Blue Wilderness. All the monsters in our stories come from there.

"Do not pass the great cliff and cross into the open ocean," Greatmother would warn us season after season. "No orca who goes into the wild ever comes home."

"This way," I say to Deneb, turning us away from danger. He does not argue.

All three of us hurry back to the sunlit plains along the coast. We sleep at last, Deneb bobbing along on one side of me and the stranger on the other.

The Pull gives way to Push, and the sun warms the water. I have never been so weary or dozed for so long. My muscles relax. My many nicks and

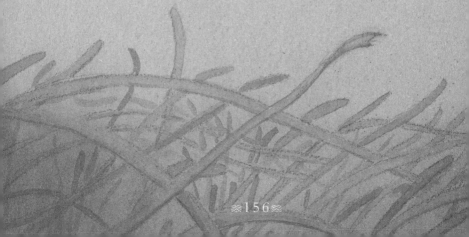

cuts bleed and then mend, making a whole piece of my skin. All through my dozing, I keep a flipper on Deneb so he does not stray. With every breath, I listen for my mother's voice. Because Mother should be here where Greatmother said we must go. But all I can hear is the faint pop and crackle of fish and the long, steady *shoosh* of waves on the shore.

I shake off sleep and search for my family with my click-stream. Greatmother said she would bring the family here, but I do not see them anywhere. My heart sinks. The Salish Sea is a tiny cove compared to the whole ocean.

"How will I ever find you?" I say aloud.

Deneb murmurs, bumps up against me, sighs,

and goes back to sleep. I stroke his back and watch over him. Wherever my family has gone, I know one thing for certain; they will never stop looking for me.

The sun climbs the sky. Everywhere I look, the coastline is a jumble. Trees lean at wrong angles or lie flat on the ground. Boats are broken on the rocks. Small fish that are usually tucked into little crevices of rock circle in the open. Bottom dwellers swim in the pale green sunlit waters, waiting for the muck and sand to settle. The big whales and porpoises that made the sprint to the ocean with us are long gone.

I double back. I check for my family again. And with each empty echo that returns to me, I feel a pulse of guilt. I left them—in the saddest moment of our lives.

Deneb finally wakes up. "Where's Mother?"

I cannot bring myself to say, *I do not know.* Mother never said it, certainly not Greatmother. A wayfinder should know.

"Where's Greatmother? Where's Uncle Rigel...."

Deneb goes through every name in our kinship. I count breaths, slowly, as I have seen Mother do many times before.

"We will just have to wait ... umm ... for the water to clear."

Why did I say that? Our family could be anywhere. Clear water is not going to make them appear.

"Okay," Deneb says cheerfully.

He nudges the stranger, who opens his sleeping eye.

"We're looking for our family," Deneb says. "Are you looking for yours?"

The stranger grunts and lifts his head out of the water.

"Where's your mother?" Deneb goes on, popping up beside him. "And your Greatmother? You won't last long without them."

He says it with such confidence; my heart aches. It is all my fault. I stole Capella's body. I only

thought of my own feelings. And little Deneb—
only twenty seasons old—came to find me. It is my
fault we are lost.

The stranger swims toward the island and the
dozing seals on the rocky shore. A mother seal
basks in the sun beside her baby.

I feel a pang of envy.

Who will shelter me

now? Nobody. I look at Deneb. I am only twenty-four seasons older, but he is mine to feed and protect now. I'm all the mother he has.

Deneb chats on and on to the stranger. "Uncle Rigel said Vega and I would find each other, and we did! I bet your sister is already looking for you. . . . You have to trust your sister, Uncle Rigel says. . . . She could be just around the next island. . . . Vega knows what to do."

I count breaths again, to hold back the panic.

They cannot be far. I lift my head above the skin of the sea and circle slowly. There are no net

boats in sight. Not one. The big thing carriers are gone. Plumes of smoke swirl up from the shore.

I strive to be as serene as Mother would be. I turn coldward. Shape my click-stream for maximum distance and send it out. A pulse of sound. And

then another. As I wait for the echoes to come back, Deneb is still chatting at the silent stranger.

"Which way do you think your mother would go?" he says. "Are you hungry? Are there fish? Are there salmon?"

I begin to appreciate how often my family divided up Deneb's questions so nobody had to answer them all.

"Do you suppose they're still back there?" Deneb asks. He looks into the passage, where a thing carrier has its nose pointing down and its tail end in the air.

"We have to leave the Salish Sea," I say. "The blood of boats is poison to us."

"But what if our family is back there?" Deneb says. "In all that . . . broken everything. We have to find them!"

"No," I say firmly, trying my best to sound like a true wayfinder. "The sour taste of boat blood will come. Our eyes will sting and grow blurry. Poison is spreading in our home waters and boats are going upside down and whole cliffsides and trees are falling in. We have to go!"

I face the ocean. It spreads before us, big as the sky.

CHAPTER SIXTEEN
SEAL

Vega is searching for the right way to go. She is thinking a wayfinder's thoughts.

I shouldn't pester her. Luckily, I'm good at being patient.

The stranger waits too. I'm sure his mother will come for him soon.

I'm much too big to complain, but waiting would be better if there was food.

"Are you hungry?" I say to the stranger. "Do you ever eat fish?"

He doesn't answer but swims slowly along the rocky edge of an offshore island.

"I think we should find something to eat. How about flat fish?"

Still no answer.

I keep trying. "Maybe we could try eels? Do you think we should hunt an octopus?"

Turns out there are a lot of things the stranger doesn't eat. He continues his silent search. And I follow him, always staying in Vega's sight.

Most of the kelp forest has been ripped away. But the few kelp trunks left bend oceanward in the Pull.

"Hey, look!" I call to the stranger. "Otters!

Do you eat those? They're kind of small."

I point my click-stream at a pair of otters who are floating on their backs in the drifting fronds of kelp. They both drop their clams and roll belly down. They swim toward the rocks; their bodies ripple like eels. They turn sideways and slip through a crevice into a sheltered pool. They pop up and hiss at me.

"Caught them!" I shout. "They're right here. I'm good at the finding game. See!"

The stranger blows a short bubble stream; probably he is thanking me. I turn back to my quarry, full of pride. I check the narrow crevice that leads to the rocky pool. There isn't a spot wide enough for me. Only my flipper will fit.

"You can just eat them when they come out," I explain. "They'll be hungry soon." I settle in to

watch and wait. My empty stomach roars like a sea lion. The otters dive. One picks up a rock. It has human-shaped front flippers with grabbers. It holds the rock and bangs it against some mussels, breaking a few free. The other otter breaks off barnacles. The pair of them float belly up. They crack the shells and slurp out the luscious middles. There's actually quite a lot of food in that tiny pool. I feel the shine of my game go a little dim. The stranger turns away, silent as always, and heads down the coast toward the next cluster of rocks.

Vega swims to my side.

"The stranger needs to hunt," she says. "He's hungry just like you."

"I know. I was helping."

"The Seal-eating Kinship has their own ways," she says. We swim along the coast, giving the stranger plenty of space. "They hunt by stealth."

"Stealth? What's that?"

"They go quiet, using neither their voices nor their click-streams, only their eyes."

I follow Vega as she lifts her head above the water and scans the shore. I can hardly believe what she has said.

"How do they find things?"

"Well, the otters got away because they heard you," Vega says. "Seals and sea lions hear just the same."

"No!"

"Yes."

"They have ears?"

"They do."

We duck underwater, travel farther, and pop up again for another look. Broken trees and an overturned net boat litter the sand. Dead fish lie in the sun. I think about the stranger and our time together.

"So when I talk to him and he doesn't answer, it's because . . ."

"Stealth," Vega says gently. "He is trying to hunt."

"I don't think I'd be very good at stealth," I mumble. "It seems kind of lonely to me."

Vega strokes me with her flipper. "I'm right here," she says. "I'll always talk to you. But we should let the stranger hunt and not frighten away his food. It's only fair. He helped us."

I want to do right by the stranger. I want to be strong and fat and confident like him. I want to learn all the things he knows. But he is not going to explain things. I follow anyway, to learn what I can by watching.

Vega keeps going along the coastline, muttering to herself about way markers. I thought there was a river by this beach, but nothing looks like I remember. I'm so glad wayfinding is her work and not mine.

The stranger is just ahead of us. We swim past rocky shorelines and sandy ones. Logs and branches and even whole trees float by. I'm too hungry to play with them. Vega searches for salmon, but she doesn't call me to hunt with her. The day moves to dark. Pull gives way to Push, and my hunger grows. I start looking for flat fish, spiky fish, tiny fish. Anything.

The stranger slows as we come to the next group of rocks. The Push lifts seals off the rock. They swim away in clusters of two and three. The stranger hangs in the water, barely breathing—he's so quiet. I hold my breath and watch him.

And then when a seal leaves the rock alone, the stranger lunges for him, mouth open like a gulper. He gets his teeth around the tail of the seal and bites deep. The seal grunts out a panicked cry, and the other seals scatter.

The stranger arches out of the water and swings the seal over his head. The seal bellows in rage as it flies through the air and smacks the water. The cries of the seal abruptly stop. The stranger swings the seal through the air one more time, and as it hits the water, I click-stream it furiously to see what has happened. The big middle bone that runs through the center of the seal is broken. The stranger lets go of the tail end and bites into the neck. Blood swirls out. I watch the seal's breathing parts fill with water and its heart slow and shudder to a stop.

I love to hunt. Nothing feels better than chasing salmon and catching them. Bringing a salmon to my sister and mother, especially to my greatmother, is the best feeling ever. But I have never watched a creature who breathes air like me be hunted. Not close up. The stranger is incredible. I can't wait to be as strong as him. But even though a seal looks different on the outside, I can't help but see how

much it looks like me on the inside. For the first time, I feel a twinge of fear as I watch the stranger.

He bites and shakes the seal. Lets it go and bites again. At first it seems mean to keep biting a seal that is already dead. But then I see that the stranger is trying to break off a piece to eat.

"Let me help you," I say.

I take the seal's tail in my teeth and hold firm. The stranger pulls against my grip and tears off a mouthful. He makes a warm and happy hum as he gulps in his food. When he has eaten his fill, he nudges a chunk toward me.

I eye it carefully. Seal isn't something I've been given by my mother or greatmother. But I'm so hungry. Vega is still searching for salmon. The tips of her flukes are making that nervous twitch she gets when she's trying to stand up to Aquila. She *will* find food. The wayfinder always does. But I'm hungry now.

I take a nibble. The furry bits are awful, but the meat is savory. The stranger turns away from me.

I try to spit out all the pointy bits while he's not watching. It's harder than it looks. My throat burns when I swallow. My stomach aches. The stranger swims away, and I am too miserable to ask him to stay. I let the rest of the seal's tail drop to the ocean bottom, where crabs and eels will pick it clean. I watch the stranger swim out of sight, wondering if I will ever see him again.

I circle back to Vega's side. She is deep in her wayfinder thoughts, click-streaming the shore over and over. I give her a nuzzle.

"Are you all right?" she says. "Did the stranger hurt you?"

"I'm fine."

My belly makes a noise. A loud noise.

"What did you eat?"

"Nothing."

I squirm as my belly makes another even louder noise. Vega turns her click-stream toward me and gives me a gentle but searching look from nose to fluke.

"You ate seal," she says.

I move away from her. My stomach feels bad, very bad. A long and loud and blood-tinged squirt comes out my back end.

"I was helping him," I say.

We both swim away from my squirt, but another just as loud and bloody follows.

"I was hungry. I thought seal would be good to eat because the stranger ate it."

"Their ways are not our ways," Vega says. "No amount of trying will make us alike."

My flukes and flippers droop. "Where did our salmon go?"

I shouldn't ask her those things. I should trust her. But I'm so hungry. I've never been hungry like this before. "Did I do something wrong?" I whisper. "Is it my fault they're gone?"

Vega strokes my head. I am sick again. We move out of the bay and into clear water. I let the roll of the ocean soothe me.

"If all the orca ate salmon, there would not be

enough for everyone," Vega begins. "So some orcas eat seals, to keep the balance. They are not kin, but we help each other by keeping to our own food and our own ways."

My belly is finally empty; I don't even try to stop moaning. Vega explains that the salmon were scattered by the big waves. I'm not listening. After a while she stops explaining things and swims beneath me. She clicks tenderly all along my aching belly.

"I will find you food," Vega croons to me. "I promise."

"I won't eat seal ever again!" I have never been more sorry in my life. I close an eye and fall asleep. Even in my dreams I am hungry.

CHAPTER SEVENTEEN
LOST

How could I have promised him food? What was I thinking? I have no idea where the salmon are. None! I rock from side to side. I make the soft whistle my mother crooned to me when I was a youngling. How am I going to take care of Deneb *and* find salmon? I stopped watching him, just for a moment, and he ate wrong food.

Also, I cannot believe how much I sound like Aquila. I swore I would never be like her, but the

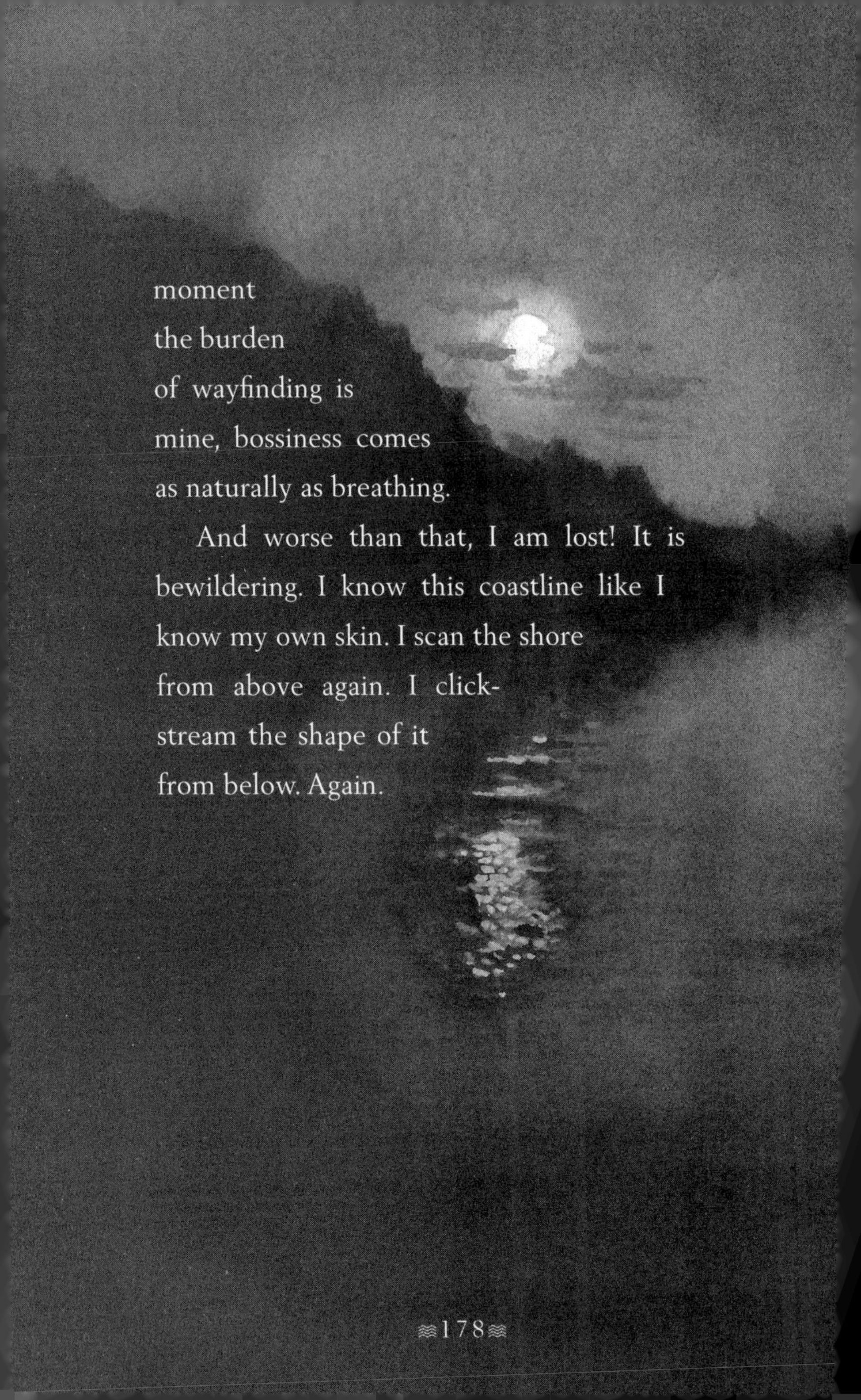

moment
the burden
of wayfinding is
mine, bossiness comes
as naturally as breathing.

    And worse than that, I am lost! It is
bewildering. I know this coastline like I
know my own skin. I scan the shore
from above again. I click-
stream the shape of it
from below. Again.

The island with the light at the mouth of the Salish Sea, I tell myself, *and then warmward along the coast to the bay with a river at each end, where the salmon come when the trees go yellow.*

None of that is before me. Yet I have traveled the outer coast many times before. The beach is unnaturally wide. Long amber trunks of kelp lie tangled on the wet sand alongside fish of all sizes. Crabs scuttle around and through the flotsam, waving their claws as if to scold the water for going so far away. The trees on the far edge of the sand are stripped of their bark and branches.

Snowcapped eagles circle above and then settle on the sand, walking from one feast to the next. After a whole night of searching, I find one flat fish. I take a bite and bring the rest to Deneb.

"How is your belly now?"

"Empty," Deneb says, still drowsy.

"Take this."

I pass him the flat fish. I have to give him

something. A wayfinder feeds her family. And today I am all Deneb has.

"Follow me. We have to keep moving."

"I'm beside you," Deneb answers, sleepy but earnest.

My heart aches remembering Uncle Rigel, who always says the same. How could I have left him?

We swim along the shore all that day and

into the night. This coastline was our winter playground. We hunted salmon at the mouths of the rivers. Shouted into sea caves to hear the echo. Dared each other to swim through stone arches.

The arches are toppled now, and the caves are filled with the skeletons of the forest. And the rivers . . . the rivers that feed us are choked with mud.

Deneb keeps to my side all through the night. As the sun rises, a song comes from the forest. It is like the song of the whales, rising and falling, louder and then softer. We stop to listen.

"Who is that?" Deneb asks.

Humans sometimes walk the beaches with a creature on the end of a line that sings like this. But not exactly like this. This is a wilder sound. I cannot help but think the land creature, whoever it is, wants to tell me something.

The voice sings and stops. Sings and stops.

As though it is calling to family—calling and hearing no answer. I remember what Greatmother said about the last time the sea shook with such violence. Hard times followed for every creature.

Deneb snuggles up to me. "It sounds lonely," he says.

I do not say it aloud, but I am sure the voice is grieving for its lost world. I want to howl too. I want to cry for everything I have lost. But that would frighten Deneb, and he is trying so hard to be brave.

I am trying too. There is no food here on the winter hunting grounds. But I cannot give up. I will not. I have to try the one place Greatmother told me never to go. There is nowhere else to turn.

"Follow me," I command.

CHAPTER EIGHTEEN
BLUE WILDERNESS

I turn away from the rising sun, and Deneb follows me. The bottom of the ocean slopes downward. Channels wind across it like the branches of a huge tree. The slope goes to a cliff and then plunges down, past where light can reach. The cold of the deep flows upward. I shiver. This is the boundary Greatmother warned me never to cross.

The Pull is with us. Deneb and I speed over the edge, trying not to think about the fearsome stories we both remember. I click-stream furiously ahead, looking for—I know not what. Monsters.

Or worse, the desolate Blue Wilderness far from the sound of waves breaking on the shore.

I swim steadily all through the day and into the night, and Deneb sticks to my side like a shadow. I pause to rest as the sun rises. I float tail down and flippers flat on the top of the water, so that I rise and fall with the long swells that are the heartbeat of the ocean. I turn in every direction. No land is in sight. Nothing but the endless gray-blue of the sea. The pale blue of the sky and its cloud islands stretch just as vast and lonely above me.

Deneb bobs on the swells beside me. He gapes at the endless horizon. Ordinarily he would be pelting me with questions, but now he only spins in slow circles, looking and looking and looking at . . . nothing.

He sighs and rubs his head against my chin without saying anything at all. I cannot think what to say either. Everything I worried about in my home waters seems small compared to the open ocean. Deneb slips beneath the swells. He holds still—a stillness as strange as our surroundings.

"Difficult to find your way in the wild," Greatmother warned me when I was a youngling with a taste for monster stories.

"The Blue Wilderness is no place for us," Mother said when I dared Aquila to swim over the edge all those seasons ago.

Beneath the water, it is not quite so barren as the surface—a faraway growl from a boat on one side of us, the high-pitched chatter of a dolphin family on another side. But there is no scuttle and crunch from crabs and sea stars and urchins. I shape a long-distance click and aim it down into the dark. Ten heartbeats pass before the echo of the sloping

ocean bottom returns to me. The thought of all that water and all the nameless silent fishes that lurk there makes me shudder.

"I'm beside you," Deneb says. He rests his flipper on mine. "I'm right here."

I turn my thoughts to the swells around me. The sun rises over land; it will show me the way home. I am not lost. Not completely. I rest with my breather above the water and the sun warming my back.

"Home is toward sunrise," I say to Deneb, putting all of my pretend confidence in my voice. "We can go home whenever we want. But we will search here for the fish that have left the coast." I say it like Aquila would, steady and strong, like Mother and Greatmother would. Like a command that nobody would think to disobey.

"I'm with you," Deneb says, sounding more confident too. "What will we eat?"

That is the heart of it.

"Salmon come from the ocean," I say firmly. "They must be here somewhere."

I examine the water for things the size and shape of a grown salmon. With no islands or seamounts or even wrecks to gather around, fish are few and most of them small. I spend all day and long into the night searching for a meal. Deneb searches too. Sometimes he points out a fish with his click-stream.

"This one?" he says. "Is this one safe?"

But they are all too small, or have a wrong-shaped tail, or a spiny ridge. Some fish are poison. Even a youngling knows it. And every poison fish has pretenders who look dangerous but are delicious, and so every youngling learns to look carefully and only eat the ones you are sure about. But as the day wears on and my hunger grows, I start to think about trying a new fish—trying, and risking my life.

As the sun sets, Deneb and I come across a swarm of something tiny and pink in the water. Larger fish are eating the tiny pink things, and some of them are salmon size!

"There!" Deneb shouts. "We can eat them! Right?"

I examine the fish closely. They are not quite right in the tail shape, and the curve of the gills is wrong too. But they look so good, so almost right.

"Yes. Let's give them a try."

We move into position, me circling down to drive the fish up, Deneb waiting at the surface to grab them. Out of the depths a long and deep

humming moan drifts toward us. Deneb darts to my side, blasting his click-stream furiously at the new sound. It is a low and slow sound. A thrumming that grows louder. I hurry Deneb away from the bait cloud and we watch, silently, so the humming creature will not find us.

An enormous whale swims into view. It is

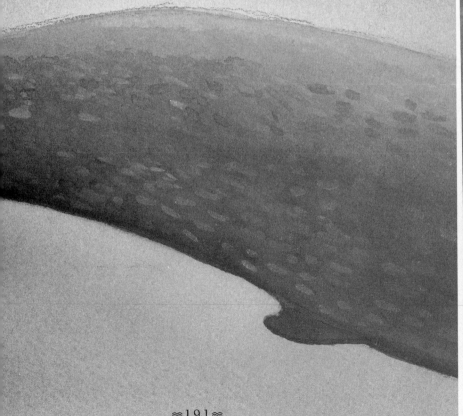

minke shaped, with the long grooves under the chin that all gulper whales have, but this one is bigger than a minke, bigger than a singing whale. It is long and strong, with blue-gray speckled skin.

"Wow!" Deneb whispers as the whale passes by.

Even Uncle Rigel, biggest of us all, would be small as a herring next to this whale. It keeps going, looking neither to one side nor the other. The fish eating at the bait cloud flee into the shadows. The

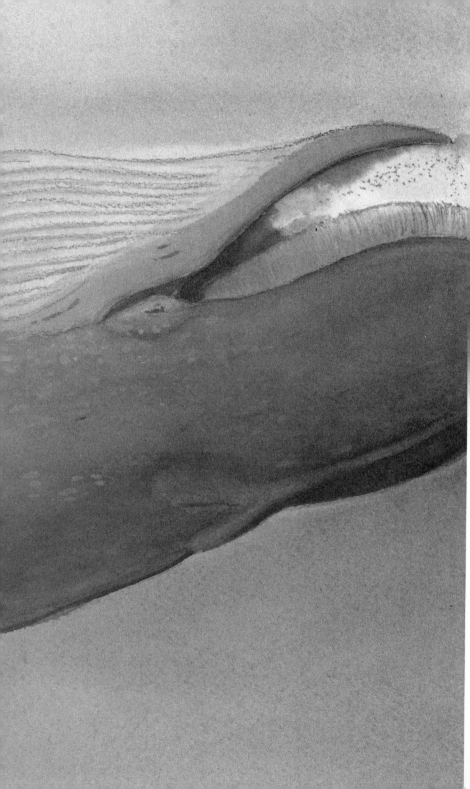

whale does not lunge. It merely opens its great mouth, chin billowing outward, and then closes it. A second gulp and then a third follow. The bait cloud is down to a few scattered pink things. The larger hunting fish are nowhere to be seen.

But I cannot think about that now. I am filled with wonder at what we have seen. Mother and Greatmother have never told me about this creature. I gaze at him, committing every detail to memory. I will tell of this moment for the rest of my life—this meeting with the king, the Chinook of whales.

"Wow," Deneb says as the whale disappears from view. "Wow. Wow!" he shouts. He circles me and then leaps clear of the water. "That was *amazing*!"

I feel the fizz of bubbles against my skin. "A lucky sign," I say. "We will find our family. And we will find our salmon too. I know it."

I lift my head to the darkening sky. My name star shines above me. I am a world away from my home waters, but she is as bright and blue as ever. Deneb's star follows mine over the arch of the sky. I drink in the beauty of them both. And it does fill me up, as Greatmother said it would. The shaking of the sea has thrown everything I know out of shape. I am still scrambling to make sense of it. But the sky is bigger than any wave. It has a steady strength that endures.

I will find the way. I must.

CHAPTER NINETEEN
VANISHED KINSHIP

The king of whales disappears into the blue-green haze. Incredible! I thought the stranger was big, but this whale is huge! I wish the stranger was still with us, so that he could see it. I hope someday I'll find him again, so I can tell him about it. I have never felt so small in my life. But this kind of small doesn't feel bad. Because even though the open ocean is lonely and full of emptiness, it must be a good place if a whale as amazing as that lives here. We are going to be okay, Vega and me. I am not afraid.

I admit it. I had a moment of doubt when she led us into the path of a human carrier. But I was wrong about her. So wrong. She's the only wayfinder, of them all, brave enough to try the depths—the depths!—of the Blue Wilderness. No shape of a familiar shore to guide her, but she knows where to go, like the wayfinders from the old stories.

Aquila's afraid of depths, though she'd never admit it. Even Mother and Greatmother don't stray past the edge. And now I've seen something that even Uncle Rigel, for all his age and bigness, has never seen. Already I'm making up a story about it!

I swim at Vega's side all night long. We doze together when the sun is high in the sky and keep going long after dark. Vega will find our family. Uncle Rigel promised she would.

I'm hungry, but I'm much too big to complain about it. So I don't. Not one bit. It's exhausting not to. So exhausting it's making me hungry. But Vega *will* find me salmon. I know she will. They have to be here somewhere.

I did think there'd be crowds of fish in the wild. I thought there would be whales everywhere and dolphins and orcas too. I thought maybe the stranger would follow us. But every time I turn to look, he is still not there. He must have found his mother and sisters. I listen for him anyway, but all I can hear is the distant rumble of big ships and the faint crackle of little fish eating littler fish and the constant rush of wind picking up water, shaping it into crests and then curls and then the froth and bubble of waves.

I blast a click-stream downward. I wait for the echo and wait . . . and wait. Nothing. My clicks are swallowed up in the dark water below us. I roll over and over in the splash of waves. It tickles nicely but does nothing to scrape the itchy bits off my skin.

"Do you see that?" Vega says suddenly. "Help me listen."

I add my clicks to her stream. In the returning echoes we see orca shapes. Many of them.

Our family survived! Made the sprint for deep water and lived! Relief swoops over me like a flying bird. They lived. They lived!

I head toward the distant orca at top speed. But Vega stays put. Ugh! How could she? I blow out a long string of impatient bubbles. And then I circle back so Vega can lead me to them.

But she doesn't. She holds very still and listens some more.

What is she waiting for? I start toward our family again, but she still doesn't come after me and take the lead. I blow a hurry-up bubble stream at her.

But Vega still waits.

I count my breaths as I've seen Mother do before. Vega worries. Maybe she thinks some fearsome monster is out there. But what if we get stuck? What if she gets too scared to go anywhere? If she can't find me food, the hunger sickness will take me.

My family always thinks I'm not listening because, to be fair, I'm often talking. But I do listen. Even when they think I'm playing. Four seasons ago I overheard the whole story of Triton and his mother. She got tangled in a net, and he couldn't work her free. She sank, and there was no one to help him find food. By the time Greatmother Io arrived, Triton was already terribly thin. His head took a wrong shape. He forgot how to hunt; he forgot how to swim straight and say his name and the names of his family. They fed him every bit of salmon they could find, but it was a lean year and it was too late. After many days, Triton forgot how to open his breather. He sank too.

I know that every living thing sinks in the end. There's something magnificent about the way a greatmother sinks, by the light of the round moon, in the hushed moment between Push and Pull,

with her kinship gathered around her, chanting her name. No, I'm not afraid of sinking. But to forget things—how to hunt, how to speak. That's a terrible end. I shiver and huff out a sharp breath to send the thought out of my head.

Vega is holding completely still. Except for the nervous twitch she has at the corners of her flukes. "She is wiser than she knows," Uncle Rigel said. It's true. But she doubts herself. She hesitates. I want to shout at her. *Just pick something!*

But Uncle Rigel never shouts. Uncle Antares doesn't either. I nudge Vega to rise with me. I breathe slowly and deeply so that she will too. I hum the tuneless thrum that Uncle Rigel so often croons when Greatmother is reading the night sky or feeling the currents of the sea. I rub my head against the tenderest spots on Vega's chin.

"I'm beside you," I say. "Always."

She breathes, and then she decides.

"We'll go a little closer," she says.

So we do. Advancing ever closer, all through

the dark of the night. Each time we look, the echoes are more and more perfectly orca shaped. Each time there are more of them—more than our entire kinship.

"Are they seal eaters, like the stranger?"

"I don't think so," Vega says. "We have not seen any seals or sea lions in the Blue Wilderness. Not one. Besides, they are talking a lot, just like we do."

"What are they saying? Will they hurt us?"

"No," Vega says firmly. "There is a treaty among orcas, older than ice. No orca may sink a tooth into another, nor hold her breather under water. This is not our way."

It's true. Nobody nibbles me, even when I deserve it.

"Who are they? I thought no orca could live in the open ocean."

"I wonder," Vega murmurs. "Could they be the Vanished Ones? Many seasons ago, when I wanted to swim over the edge, Greatmother told me a story about a family from our own kinship many generations ago, who strayed into the wild and never came back."

"Do you think this is them?"

"Let's find out." Vega clears a bubble from her breather and calls out. "I am Vega, daughter of Arctura, greatdaughter of Siria, of the Warmward Kinship of Salmon Eaters."

All the orca turn as one and look at us. A great wave of clicks flies in our direction. I want to hide behind Vega, but then, remembering Uncle Rigel, I move beside her, flipper touching flipper.

"I am Deneb . . ." A nervous bubble slips out. "Deneb, brother of Vega, son of Arctura and greatson of Siria, of the Kinship of Warmward Salmon Eaters." My heart pounds as loud as my voice.

One of the females, the sleekest and fattest of them all, swims forward. She is flanked on both sides by males with fins that tower over mine.

She begins to speak, slowly, as though she is telling a story to a youngling. I try to understand, but in the end I trust Vega to work out the meaning, one wayfinder to another. The mothers come forward first and speak a word into the space between us. The brothers speak after the sisters, and then the younglings and babies chirp what must be their names.

I listen carefully. One youngling says his name over and over. Just like Altair always does. I quietly give it a try. I practice, and then I say it out loud. The baby squeaks with delight, swims up to me, and blows a baby-sized bubble under my chin. I pick the little one up with my nose and give him a zoom in circles around his own mother. A pleased hum rises from the Vanished Ones.

"It is all right," Vega calls to me. "We're allowed to travel with them."

But I'm already gone, swimming after the youngling, copying his noises as we leap out of the water side by side.

CHAPTER TWENTY
HUNT

I swim among the new orcas, relieved to have other wayfinders nearby. I wish I could understand them, but even so, I can hardly believe my luck. The Vanished Ones out of legend—who else could they be? An ancient story come to life. And there are so many of them! More than my whole kinship. They have babies and younglings, not just Deneb's new friend, but many more. I feel a twinge of envy.

When I first heard about Mother's sister and

cousins who were captured all those years ago, I made up stories about them for myself. About all the babies they would have had—my cousins. I chose secret names for them. Sometimes when I played, my imaginary cousins crowded around me, loud and loving and mine. I am too old for the game now—but not too old to miss my cousins who were never born.

I watch the youngling females. Notice how they shadow their bigger sisters. Hear their lively chatter. See how they stroke each other for comfort as they swim. I miss Capella as intensely as the moment I let her body go. And I am angry that the pain and loss of those long-ago captures are not over. Not for me. Not for my entire kinship.

I wish I could talk to my new companions. I am full to bursting with questions. I try a few words, easy ones, and get no response. I listen and listen, but I cannot piece together what they are saying. I want to learn, but I am afraid to make a mistake. Still, the Vanished Ones do not shun me. They allow Deneb and me to swim among them as if we are family, and I am grateful.

We travel at a steady pace. The water itself draws us along—a current like the daily Push and Pull, but steady and flowing always in the same direction. Perhaps my family is in the same current, looking for me. I listen for them as we travel, and dream of them when we stop to doze.

When the half-moon rises, the Vanished Ones move on. They spread out as they swim. They take turns making swim shadows for their younglings and the older one with the broken flipper who cannot swim as fast as the rest. They whistle to each other to keep the huge group together.

When their clicks light up a big shape ahead of us, I feel a hum of excitement run through the entire group. They take off at top speed.

"A hunt!" Deneb calls. "A hunt at last!"

His little friend hangs back with his mother, but Deneb sprints ahead.

"Be careful!"

My voice is lost in the excitement of the hunt. I click-stream along with the rest, looking for the shapes of fish, hoping for salmon, but willing to eat whatever they will help me find.

We speed along at the surface. Ahead I see a swirl of little fish, feeder fish, the kind that salmon eat. Yes! Salmon at last!

As we get closer, I see bigger fish stalking the edges of the swirling bait cloud. They are much too large for salmon, and something is wrong with their tails. The bottom half is the regular shape and the top half is long and thin, like a giant eel. They swim up to the edge of the fish swarm and smack

it with their tails. I see one lift its head and eat the stunned fish. It has a moon-shaped mouth. A shark! There are sharks aplenty in our home waters, but none with this long tail. I have never heard of sharks like these, not even in stories.

The wayfinder dives, and all of her biggest sisters dive with her. They swim below the sharks

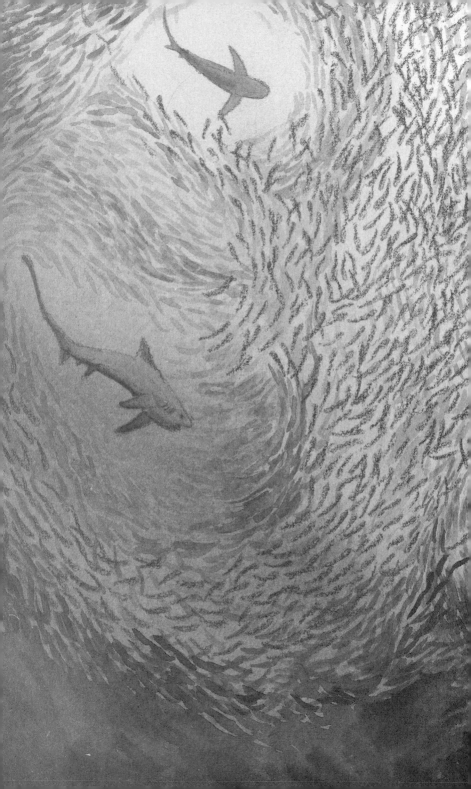

and drive them up to the surface. The sharks are swift and strong. They leap clear of the water, their tails trailing behind them. The hunters leap after them.

Feeder fish scatter as the Vanished Ones attack the sharks. But these sharks are no easy prey.

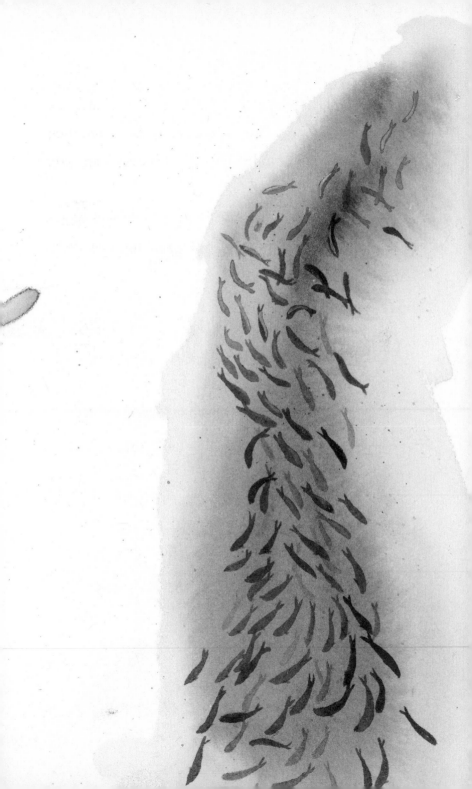

They are quick to turn and lash back. I am shocked to see the slash of a tail leave bloody marks on flippers and flukes.

Still, the wayfinder is a brilliant hunter. She presses a shark upward, and one of her sisters breaches above it and comes crashing down right on top of it. There is a great crunch, and the shark stops moving.

On my other side, another of the mothers has a shark by the fin. She swings its body through the air so that it smacks hard against the water. One of the uncles sinks his teeth into its head, while another bites the base of the tail. Blood dims the water.

"Deneb! Where are you?"

And then a shark below me swerves upward, tail lashing from side to side. It heads straight for me. I leap out of the water. But when I come down, the shark is right in front of me. I jump again, looking for an escape. All around me, the ocean is bubbling with the attack, and I am at the center of the storm.

"I'm here!" Deneb squeaks. He smashes into the shark with all his strength.

The shark spins, slashes, and then abruptly goes still as two of the Vanished Ones bite deep into its side. A moment of thrashing, and it is all over. The remaining sharks dive together for the safety of dark water and leave the Vanished Kinship to feast on their take.

My heart pounds wildly. Blood and shimmering bits of shark skin drift in great clouds around me.

"They eat sharks," I murmur, amazed.

Deneb swims up to me with a chunk of shark in his mouth.

"Try it!" he says. "I know you're hungry."

We don't eat sharks, is what I almost say. We have never eaten them before. But here we are. In the wild. With nothing else to eat. And I have never been so hungry. I dread the very thought of hunger sickness. How will I take care of my brother if I grow so thin I cannot even remember my own name? I look anxiously at him, so lean where he should be plump.

"It looks delicious," I lie, and take the bite Deneb offers.

He circles back to a carcass and tears off more. We both chew and chew. And chew.

"It's . . . crispy on the outside," Deneb says, also lying.

The shark skin grates against my teeth like a mouthful of sand. It hurts my tongue as I push the chunk out of my mouth. I glance at the Vanished Ones, who are gulping down great mouthfuls with cheerful abandon. How do they do it?

"Don't eat the skin," I say to Deneb. "Remember how the fur of that seal made you bleed inside? The shark skin will be worse."

Deneb is still chewing. He swims more slowly. I hold the gritty skin in my teeth and turn the softer meat toward him. He takes a bite, and then another.

"Better," he mumbles. "Much better."

He lolls near the surface. I tear off more and feed it to him.

"Will you hold a piece for me now?" I ask after

Deneb has eaten his fill. I should not have to ask.

"Hmm." Deneb sounds almost sleepy. I nudge him, and he grips the food by the rough side so that I can eat the good parts. It is not as oily rich as salmon, but I am not complaining. When I come back to Deneb for another mouthful, he is dozing.

"Deneb! I fed you!"

Deneb startles awake. Gives me a truly remorseful look and then dozes off again while I am still trying to eat. The chunk of food he is holding falls away into the depths.

"Hey!" I shout. "We're a family. We are supposed to help each other!"

He closes his eyes.

"Are you even listening?"

I poke him in the side. A burst of blood flows into the water from his other side.

"Deneb?"

I frantically click-stream his whole body. I swim to his other side.

"Deneb!"

There is a long curving gash below his flipper. It flaps open and shut with the roll of the ocean.

"No, no! What have you done?"

I press my body against his wound, holding it shut.

"I saved you," Deneb says. "Like Uncle Rigel would."

"You should have told me you were hurt!"

"I was hungry."

"What have I done?" I whisper. "Oh, what am I going to do?"

I press against his wound, holding the edges together. I move him to clear water, away from the blood that brings sharks and trouble. I am not strong enough for trouble. Still I watch for it. The Vanished Kinship finish their feast and move on without us. I stay at Deneb's side through the setting of the moon and the rising of the sun. I stay with him all day until the sun sets and the moon shines down on us, two lonely creatures like little stars in the boundless sky. In the darkness I sense

something large and stealthy watching us. Silently.
But when I turn to look, I see only shadows.

Nothing hunts us, I tell
myself. *Nothing hunts us.*
Mother promised. But
I do not know if her
promises hold true so far
from home.

I tell every story I can
remember, except for the ones
with monsters. Far beneath,
the watcher is still waiting. I
sing to Deneb as he dozes. I keep
myself awake by making
up tales about all the
unfamiliar fishes
that swim by.
I remember the
majesty of the
giant whale. I
marvel at the

delicate drifts of jellies and the dark gray birds who swim through the air on impossibly long wings. I shower Deneb's wound with my most soothing clicks, and on the morning of the second day, his skin holds fast and the shadows that circled us in the dark are gone.

"Do. Not. Go. Anywhere," I command him.

Before Deneb can say, "I promise," I am asleep.

In my dreams, I swim in the silvery green waters of my own Salish Sea. The wayfinders of my kinship are beside me. I pour out to them every question in my weary heart, and they say to me, "We are beside you. Always. Always. Always."

When I wake, I know what I must do. Know it as I know my own name.

CHAPTER TWENTY-ONE
HOMEWARD

"Deneb, we are going home."

"Home?" Deneb looks up at me. "I'm ready," he says.

Once he would have leaped and splashed and swum circles around me. Now he slips into place in my swim shadow and waits for me to lead him. The sun rises, marking the way home. I study the roll of the waves and the press of currents.

"This way," I say firmly, turning coldward and angling toward the sunrise. I do not know how long it will take or even if we are strong enough to make it all the way back. Days and days with nearly nothing to eat, and my head—my whole body— aches. But there is no food for us in the Blue Wilderness. And the truth of it all, the part I cannot bear to tell my brother, is that there might not be food for us at home either. But I will not let him sink out here in the wild, far from the Salish Sea and the bones of our ancestors. I will bring him home. I will scour the sea to feed him, and if there is nothing left, I will guard him until his last breath.

We travel all day and all through the night, fighting the current the whole time. The ocean feels empty without the Vanished Ones. The gray birds, more wing than body, soar above us. They hold their wings steady, tilting to one side and the other as the wind carries them. I wish the water was as

easy as the air, but their company encourages me. Deneb and I stop twice to doze. Weak as he is from the shark bite, he still keeps to my side without one chirp of complaint.

We keep heading toward the rising sun in the morning. In the heat of the day, we rest and let the sun warm us. We swim again as the water cools, turning our flukes to the setting sun. I hope for a clear night so I can find the moon. For the last two nights, the moon has been half full, all the light I need.

Greatmother calls the sun and the moon her older sisters, and I am grateful for their light. I am not wise enough to find my way by currents alone, as Greatmother does on foggy days. So I watch for the moon and the rising sun. I hope for clear skies, and I choose the way as best I can.

Late on our third day, the sea bottom begins to slope upward. We find a flat fish hiding in the mud. It is little more than a mouthful once we each take our share. I try to give Deneb the whole fish, but he just as stubbornly refuses my half.

"I need you," is all he says.

He has grown thinner over our journey and I stay alert for signs of hunger sickness—confusion, memory loss, and the wrong shape of the head.

No brother would dare call a sister skinny, but I hear Deneb checking my belly and sides more than once when he thinks I am not paying attention. Each time he mutters to himself, "Okay, good so far."

I am not so sure. I have never felt so weary in my life. How will I know if the hunger sickness strikes? What if I start leading my brother the wrong way? The urge to give up and go to sleep wraps around me like the tentacles of an octopus. There is nothing to do but keep going. I am too exhausted to even think about what we will find, or not find, when we get home.

As we approach the shore, I look above and below the water for way markers. Every river that flows into the ocean makes a fish tail mark in the mud. Each one has its own shape, fainter for slow-moving rivers, deeper and longer for big rivers. The entrance into the Salish Sea has the biggest fish tail of them all. The sea shake and the giant waves have changed the shape of the fish tails—some a little and some a lot. I struggle to find the way markers I knew before. I thought they would always be the same.

I am surprised when Deneb says, "Hey, isn't that the little island off Land's End?"

It is! The island is smaller than it was before. A section of cliff has fallen into the water. A flutter of fear zings through my body. I lift my head. Everywhere I turn, things look different. The shore is lined with broken trees, their bark and branches stripped away. The land-boat path is empty. A thin rime of boat blood floats on the surface, making my eyes sting. And it is quiet, so quiet I can see farther than I ever have before.

A thing carrier has its nose mired deep in the

sea bottom, its biting end up in the air. I can spot the circle-shaped teeth, not spinning but holding still. Rectangles from the top of the thing carrier are strewn across the mud in a jumble. Sometimes a thing carrier loses a few rectangles in a storm, but I have never seen so many of them break free. Already algae are claiming them. Crabs scuttle across the tops, and spiny urchins will soon follow. The tiny fishes that burrow in sand are swirling around looking for a new place to dig.

"Good luck, little sand hiders!" I call.

They feed our beloved salmon, and they are the first hopeful sign I have seen. I can actually hear a little shush of sound when the sand hiders find a gravelly spot they like and dive in tail first. I have seen it many times, but never heard it. I cannot resist; I follow the tiny fish away from the heap of rectangles. *Swoosh, swoosh.* I can hear the faint whisper of each one. Incredible!

Deneb follows me faithfully. "Are we going to eat those little guys now?" he says, trying hard, and failing completely, to be enthusiastic.

"Of course not!" I shake off my embarrassment. "Don't be silly."

I click-stream in a big circle. It is uncanny. There are no net boats, no watcher boats. Even the tiny growlers that fly through the air leaving a cloud stripe behind them are gone.

"What happened to the humans?" Deneb asks. "Did they disappear?"

"Maybe they are frightened, like the sand hiders," I say. "Maybe they are hiding too."

I think long and hard about our salmon. It is still the season when the mountains call them home. Will they come this year? If the net boats stay ashore, there will be more salmon for us. Maybe.

"We will find the Gathering Place," I decide. "If any of our kinship are still in the sea, they will look for us there."

I head for the coldward side of the passage.

The Pull gives way to the Push, and we swim more quickly. Deneb is moving faster too, in spite of his wound, which must still be hurting terribly. His skin has hardened and he can push his flukes with more strength, but he needs food to get well.

"Will I have a scar?" he says, rolling to the side to give me a look. "I will! I can tell. Will it be bigger than Uncle Rigel's?"

"You will have a curved scar. Uncle Rigel's is straight," I say. I cannot believe he is proud of it! I feel awful every time I see that scar. I did not protect him. He could have sunk, out there in the wild, so far from home.

"It is quite long," I say firmly. "And deep. Nobody else in our whole kinship has a shark scar like yours."

Deneb hums as he swims, no doubt thinking about the story of his adventure and how to tell it for dramatic effect.

I have no such lightness of heart. There is no way to know if our family survived. Still, Mother could be here—our whole family could. They could be right around the next point, beyond the next island. Searching, just like me.

When the Gathering Place comes into range, I shout, "I am Vega, daughter of Arctura, greatdaughter of Siria of the Warmward Salmon Eaters."

My voice rings out in the quiet sea.

"Deneb! Brother of Vega, son of Arctura, greatson of Siria, of the Mighty Kinship of Salmon Eaters!"

His little fin breaks the surface of the sea, and he breathes out the tallest *chaaaah* he can make—like the uncles always do, to announce our presence. I could cry. He is so little, and he is trying so hard.

I lift my chin and swing it from side to side to catch the smallest sounds in the water. We are over the shallows now, and the familiar nip and nibble of crabs and urchins rises from the rocks below. A far-off moan comes from a scooper whale. I look above the water and hear seals grunting to each other on the shore. I slide back underwater, still listening.

Finally and very faintly I hear, "I am Aquila, daughter of Nova, greatdaughter of Siria."

And then, "ME! I am me!"

CHAPTER TWENTY-TWO
FOUND

"Aquila!" I shout.

I swim with all my strength, leaving Deneb behind. Not even caring that he cannot keep up. Is it really her?

When my cousin comes into sight, I leap for joy. Aquila! She is alive!

"Vega! You found us."

Aquila rubs her whole body along my side with a shiver of relief.

I look all around, but I see

only Altair. He reaches out his little flipper toward me, but I keep looking for Mother and Greatmother, Uncle Rigel, and Aunt Nova. Anyone.

"Thank you." Aquila sighs. "Thank you for coming back to me."

I return her nuzzles and keep looking for my mother. She will turn up any moment. They all will. I am sure of it. Aquila would never be so bold as to leave her family.

But all I see is Altair. He is as sleek and fat as a baby should be, but Aquila is terribly lean. The shine has gone out of her eyes. I see strings of milk dripping from Altair's mouth. Aquila has nursed him. Her son has remained strong, but at a terrible cost.

"You're here," Aquila murmurs. "I knew you'd come."

I see that she is looking over my shoulder, just as I am looking over hers. Deneb charges right into us.

"Aquila! Altair! I found you!"

He swims circles around us, gleefully smacking his tail. Altair is at his side in an instant, making big noises as best he can. Aquila keeps looking beyond them, up the passage that leads to the ocean.

"Vega?" she begins.

"It's just Deneb and me," I say softly.

I do not know what else to say. Sorry is not nearly enough. My heart aches. I have been holding on to the fragile bubble of my courage, day after weary day. I have imagined my family swimming with me. Mother's strength, Greatmother's wisdom, the courage of my aunts. I told myself that all I had to do was find them. And they would take care of everything.

"I thought our family would be with you," Aquila says.

"Me too," I answer.

Just a few seasons ago we were playmates, balancing kelp and eelgrass on our heads, daring each other to lick a squid, racing with porpoises. I start to think about the journey we have in front of us, more daring and dangerous by far than any of our childhood games. Aquila is older than me. By rights she should take the lead and make the choices, but she is shockingly thin. She does not have the strength to lead. She might not even have the strength to follow.

"Rest now," I croon as I soothe her with the most healing click-stream I know how to make.

I want to cry. I want to sleep. I want my mother! I have already done so much. I want someone else to find the way.

Altair inspects Deneb's new scar and listens with awestruck attention to the story of our adventures. I imagine Deneb in his old age—the oldest brother of a vast kinship, a towering fin, a dashing scar, maybe a bit creaky in the spine, but still spinning stories for the younglings who flock around him at every gathering. The master storyteller he will be someday is already inside him. I love him. Love him like I love the wide sea and the rising sun and my own skin and the sound of my mother's voice.

I cannot blame Aquila for giving away all she had to give. I would have done the same; any mother would. And yet I cannot hide from the truth. The hunger sickness is coming for Aquila. It is only days away. If I do not find salmon, I will lose her.

"Where did our mothers go?" I ask quietly.

"For the deep," Aquila says. "We all went but when the big waves came . . . I lost my son. . . ." Her whole body shudders at the memory of it. "I went after him. I left them behind to search. The waves came again and again, but I didn't give up."

"And you found him!" I say. "All by yourself."

"But then I couldn't find Greatmother or Aunt Arctura or Uncle Rigel. I didn't know where to go. So I found my way here."

She nods toward two pillars of rock that stand on one end of the Gathering Place. The top of one is lying in pieces on the sand below. I see bruises and rub marks where Aquila was struck with all the things the waves carried.

"I know our family will come here, if only . . ." Aquila shivers again.

"If only they survived," I say. I look around one more time, still hoping Mother and Greatmother will appear. Boulders and trees and net boats litter the bottom of the sea. The water has a sour tang.

"Where did the salmon go?" I ask.

"I don't know," Aquila moans. She rocks from side to side in her distress. "I've seen a few come from the ocean, but I'm not strong enough to hunt them, not alone. Altair is hungry. What will I do if . . ."

She cannot bear to say it, but we both know that if the hunger sickness comes, it will take her milk first, and then her memory.

"I will not let it happen," I say. I think about the day I carried my sister's body to Blood Cove. "Not today. Not ever."

Altair and Deneb are playing with a scrap of net, as carefree as younglings should be. I feel a wave of

stubbornness and pride grow in me
like a winter storm.

I will not let you sink, I
silently promise. *I will
go as far as it takes and
kill whatever I must to
keep you alive.*

I turn to Aquila, but in my
mind I see Capella as she would
have been all grown up. "You are not
alone now," I say firmly.

I circle the Gathering Place, thinking hard.
Our family must be somewhere along the coast.
Aquila would have heard them return. Especially
now that the water is quiet. I want to race back to
the ocean and find my mother and follow her lead
faithfully, as I have my whole life.

But.

Aquila is too weak for the ocean currents. Altair
and Deneb need me now. There is no one else to
lead them.

"Where will we go?" Aquila says. "Our salmon could be anywhere."

I feel my doubts growing. What if I choose wrong?

No, those doubts are a stone I do not have to carry. I cannot be timid. Not now. I have come too far for that.

"The mountains call to the salmon," I say.

I lift my head above the water and turn to the sunrise side of the sea. The mountains are still there, in spite of the shaking.

"The biggest mountain will call the loudest, just as the biggest whale has the loudest voice," I decide.

I remember a flat-topped mountain, tallest of them all, near the warmward reach of the sea. Other mountains go gray in the heat of the warm season, but this one is always whitecapped and gleaming.

"There is a mountain," I say. "Greatmother

called it the Mother of Rivers. It is the biggest one of all. We will find our salmon there."

I have made my choice, and if I chose wrong, there is no one to blame but me.

"Do you know the way?" Aquila asks. "What if we get lost?"

I call on every memory I have of the warmward waters. Salmon have always come before. Going up the rivers to the mountains is their life. I push my doubts aside and swallow my fears.

"We have to try."

"Vega is wiser than she knows!" Deneb announces, in a careful imitation of Uncle Rigel's voice. "I will follow her anywhere," he adds stoutly. He swims to my side.

"Follow! Follow!" Altair chirps. He nuzzles his mama and then cuddles up to me for good measure.

"I'm tired," Aquila says. "So tired! But if you

know the way, I
will go with you."

"The wind is at our flukes,"
I say gently. "I will not leave
you behind." I take
the wayfinder's place
and lead the remnant of my family
away from our Gathering Place and
toward the mountains—I hope. Toward
food—I hope. I am not sure about any of it. I
only know I have to try.

CHAPTER TWENTY-THREE
HUNGER

V_{ega} leads us away from the Gathering Place. Aquila slips into my usual spot in her swim shadow.

"Hey!"

I'm about to nudge her away, so we can travel like we always did before—me in Vega's shadow and Altair with Aquila. But when I come close, I see the swollen bump on her body where she was struck by something huge and heavy, and another lump farther down her back. A bruise shows on the white part of her belly.

"Hey what?" Aquila snaps, already mad at me even though I haven't done anything wrong yet.

"Umm . . . hey, Altair," I say. "Let's catch an octopus."

"Oh?" Altair looks to his mother and then back at me.

"They are very tricky to catch," I add. "And dangerous!"

"Oooh!" Altair comes to my side and immediately starts blasting his little click-stream in all directions.

"You're going to be a great octopus finder!" I tell him. I launch into my best octopus story, hoping that I have chosen the right thing—the thing that helps.

Aquila sighs, sounding more tired than mad now.

"Keep close," Vega says.

We travel slowly and rest often. I want to find the salmon now. I want to fly through the water at top speed and be there already. But my scar does not feel as great as it looks. Every downward push with my flukes makes my newly mended skin ache. And it's harder to swim with nobody bigger pulling me along in their shadow.

I sing to Altair because I need the encouragement myself. He chimes in with his little chirp, "Side by side! . . . Fin! . . . Fluke!"

Vega calls out sea marks as we go past them, but I don't recognize a single one. Old pillars have tumbled. Tangles of broken trees drift by. Giant kelp float over deep water, ripped from their holdfasts. Huge drifts of mud cover places that were rocky before. Sandy shorelines are scraped down to bare rock. Ravens and eagles and bears, the great eaters of dead things, are thick on the shore. Strangest of

all, the water is quiet. A small wind boat crosses well in front of us. A few of the dragonfly boats creep along. Nothing else is moving.

Vega and Aquila call out their names as we travel and listen for answers. At first only echoes come back. As the morning wears on, we hear a pair of dolphins and the confused grunts and huffs of seals searching for their uprooted kelp forests.

We stop at a shallow place to rest. Vega and Aquila put their heads together and talk. For once, Aquila doesn't get bossy and Vega doesn't swim off in a temper. Together they untangle our way.

I miss Uncle Rigel, more than ever. I try to be steadfast like him, a calm place in a moving sea. But I don't feel steady or strong. I can barely stay awake. Altair is weary too. He pokes at Aquila's milk spots, but nothing comes out.

"Hungreeeeee," he whines.

I hustle him away from Aquila and rock him between my flippers. He's so exhausted it only takes a moment for him to fall asleep. I doze beside him. When I wake, the sun is going down and I hear the wayfinders arguing.

"I can't," Aquila whimpers like a youngling. "I'm not strong enough."

"You are," Vega says. She makes her voice firmer and deeper, like Greatmother. "We have come so far already."

"We aren't even halfway," Aquila wails, not comforted at all. "And soon the Pull will be against us."

They can't give up! I won't let them! I wake Altair and tuck him into my swim shadow. My scar aches, but I pretend that it doesn't.

"I'm ready!" I announce. I give Altair a nudge.

"Ready," he echoes.

"See," Vega says proudly. "They're ready."

We travel on in the growing darkness, even more slowly than before.

When the Push turns to Pull, we find a quiet cove to rest in. The moon is growing rounder and brighter each night; I look on it like a promise.

There is food somewhere, and my sister will lead us to it. Vega tells me to sleep, so of course I pretend to. She checks each one of us for the signs of hunger sickness. So far we are only thin, but not wrong shaped.

Vega calls out her name to the empty sea. We both lift our chins to collect the faintest and most faraway sounds, listening for our family to call back. They don't, but even so I am proud of my sister, wayfinder of the mightiest kinship in the sea! I swim to her side and nudge her gently.

"Rest," I say. "Rest and let me watch."

To my surprise, she agrees and then falls into line with Aquila and Altair, rising and breathing as one.

I watch over my family as the moon rises big and orange. I guard them as it fades to yellow and then white. When the Pull gives way to Push, I wake them.

We swim into the long narrow channels of the warmward reach. Many humans live here and they are loud, loud, loud! But today it's spooky quiet. The places where boats nest along the shore are in shambles—one boat stacked up on another or turned upside down. Land boats are off their paths—not darting back and forth, but lying empty on their backs or sides. Usually we go quickly past the noisy piles of towering gray and black rectangles where so many of the humans live. Now the big rectangles are tilted against each other, their skins stripped away, so that you can see the rising sun through their bones. Smoke drifts up and makes a smudge across the sky.

We make our way more slowly now. I start to recognize things, the smaller bend and then the larger one with the high bridge. Eagles and hawks soar low over the water, grabbers at the ready, hunting. Aquila stops swimming altogether and lets the Push carry her. When we come to a side channel, we click-stream to look for salmon. Vega calls her name. We rest and wait for an answer.

No salmon. No answer.

Aquila sighs and says nothing. But she gives Vega

a silent nudge of encouragement, and Vega takes the lead again. Altair is so sleepy, he is zigzagging. I guide him to the middle, between me and Aquila, so he doesn't go astray. Seals swim past. Even otters are traveling more quickly than us. I hear the chitter and squeak of a porpoise. When he comes into view; his sleek gray sides are a web of nicks and cuts, but he's click-streaming for food. Trying his best, just like us.

"Good

luck, tiny whale," I say to him as he goes by.

We let the Push carry us past one island and then another.

"Almost there," Aquila says. "Can't stop now."

She gives Vega another nudge, and we keep going. At last, the Mother of Rivers appears, all crowned in snow on the horizon. There should be a prairie of eelgrass here on the soft muddy bottom where the river meets the sea. But the grass is gone. Only a few shreds of it drift and flicker in the water. The mud is scraped away, leaving a barren pebbly stretch of empty ground.

There is a swarm of something, right where the river should be. Eagles circle above it. A bull seal lion and the mothers of his family swim past us, all muscle and fang. Seals are on the move too, salmon eaters—all of them. Something is going on up there. Vega sees it too. She doesn't stop to catch her breath. She doesn't wait for Aquila.

"I am giving you a ride, Altair," Vega says.

She swoops under him and lifts him up. She speeds toward the mouth of the river.

"Are they there?" Aquila says. "Is it really true?"

"I think it's them!" I shout. "Let's go!"

We dash along side by side, all our tiredness forgotten, past the last of the islands and yes. Yes! There they are. Chinooks—kings of all salmon! Gathered in a swirling moon like giant herrings.

Vega darts into the swarm, Aquila at her side. She catches one and brings it to me to share, but I have already caught mine. A big one! I gulp down the big fish, feeling the burst of oil in my mouth, the satisfying crunch of bone, the delicious crackle of skin.

This is the food that

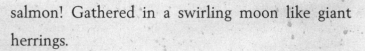

feels right in my belly. The food I was born to eat. I've never seen so many salmon in one spot. They are fat and heavy. I gorge myself, eating ten and then twenty more. Vega and Aquila do the same. We feed Altair. I grow dizzy from the feeling of being full. I knew Vega could do it, and I was right! She is the queen of wayfinders. We will never be hungry again!

CHAPTER TWENTY-FOUR
SALMON

I stop hunting for a moment, just a moment, to let out a deep *chaaaah* of gratitude. They followed me. They were more exhausted, more hurt, more sad than they have ever been in their lives. But they followed me just the same.

I thought about giving up when the way markers looked so different. I felt like giving up when we saw the kelp forests broken away from their holdfasts and the sandy beaches stripped down to bare rocks. I did not know I had the strength to keep going. But here we are. One right thing in an upside-down world.

I watch my family with a rush of pride. I found food for them—like a true wayfinder. Even Altair has made a catch of his own. We did this together! We are the youngest of our kinship, and we found our salmon! All around me, other hunters grab their share—seals, sea lions, eagles. They eat their fill, and still the salmon do not run up the river to escape. Something prickles my memory.

"Look to the water. What touches the water touches us all."

The memory of my greatmother's words rings like the warning bell. Salmon are never this easy to hunt. Something is wrong. I check the mud for the

broad fish tail that marks the river's mouth. The bottom is scraped down to bare gravel.

I look to the shore for the opening of the river. I search for the push of fresh water against my body. I lift my head above the skin of the sea. Where there was once an outlet, now there is a tangle of broken trees, boulders, and land boats.

I leap to look over the tangle. Behind it, water stretches out in a vast flat lake where there was once grass and trees and the nests of more birds than there are stars in the sky. All of it is underwater.

I turn back to the salmon, now many fewer than before. A bull sea lion bites deep into a salmon right in front of me. Its belly bursts open. A thousand red-orange eggs pour out and swirl before me like tiny bubbles. They dance for a moment in sunlit waters and then sink into the darkness.

The sight of them hits me like a bolt of lightning. Salmon go to the mountains to have their babies. They are wayfinders too. They travel out of the Blue Wilderness, across the Salish Sea and into its

farthest reach, to find the opening of this river. But now their way is blocked. No river. No babies. I feel the tug of those thousand tiny lives that will never

be born. They are not my kinship, not my family, and yet everything I love will be lost without them.

I turn in a frantic circle. Everywhere I look, salmon are being devoured.

"Deneb! Stop!"

"Stop?" Deneb says, quickly swallowing the salmon he has caught in one gulp. "Why?"

A cloud of silver scales shimmers around him. They fall through the water like rain. What have I done?

"Aquila!" I shout. But Aquila is deep in the dwindling mass of salmon, frantically eating one after another. Hunger is all she can hear.

I am sick inside, as though I have swallowed stones. "Deneb, we have to stop hunting and get these salmon to their home river. If we eat them all, they'll never have babies."

Deneb stops. He looks at me. "If you eat everything, you make a wasteland of the sea," he says. "Mother used to tell me that."

"Yes! They need the river."

"What river?"

I do not understand how this happened. But I know it is wrong. Rivers run into the sea, as constant as the stars that swim across the night sky, always in the same direction.

I leap again, to look over the barrier blocking the mouth of the river. There are boats on the vast lake, long boats, with the beak in front like a great bird. The longboat riders! They are salmon hunters too. Are they coming to take? I watch them, sick with dread.

Soon the riders are standing on the rubble. Some have sticks with a big tooth on the end. They lunge and bite at the broken trees. They clear branches away. They prod boulders free with long sticks. I have never seen humans do this work before. They are trying to open the river's mouth. But the rubble is thick and heavy, and they are only humans.

I swim along the barrier, click-streaming the sides of it. Probing for a place to break through. The rubble is thick everywhere, but some places are more rocky and some are choked with overturned land boats. Those will be hard to move. But a little farther on, I find a spot that is mostly trees with mud and sand. Trees float, and water can push away mud.

"We have to open the river!" I shout to Deneb. "Try here."

Deneb grabs a branch in his teeth. It breaks off. He tries again. It breaks again, and the trunk is still in place.

"We need help," I say.

I call Aquila's name, but she is still deep in the hunt and does not hear me. I hurry back to the humans, wondering how I will tell them to come. Nobody even agrees that humans can talk. I leap to get their attention. They look up from their work, but only for a moment.

I study them carefully and choose the one with the pearl-colored hair. The others listen to her. When she points, they go where she is pointing. A human wayfinder! Perfect!

"This way!" I call to her. "We need your help. Our salmon will die if you do not come!"

The human wayfinder does not hear me.

"Hurry!" I shout.

She keeps working with her fellow humans. I snatch a salmon by the tail and show it to her. I toss it onto the barrier in front of her. She bends down and takes the salmon in her grabbers. She carries it to the other side of the barrier and sets it tenderly in the water. Then she turns and looks me right in the eye.

I swim toward Deneb, keeping to the surface so that she can see me clearly.

She follows.

I lead her to the weak spot. I take a tree trunk in my mouth and pull. It does not budge. I put my head against it and push with all my strength. The human probes into the mud with her stick. She waves and shouts to her kinship. And they come!

I watch her as she shows the other humans where to go and what to do. Lines come out. They wrap them around the tree trunks. Several humans take hold of the lines and pull. Deneb and I go below and push. We can hear the humans chant as they work, all leaning together to give one pull the strength of many pullers.

When I come up for air, I see more boats, long and little, paddling across the flooded river. More humans join the work. Some have sticks with a raven-tail shape at the end. They push the raven-tail end into the sand and gravel and scoop up bites of the mud that holds the trees fast. The first trunk comes free, but a larger one is beneath it.

More lines. More pulling.

Deneb takes a small trunk in his teeth and wiggles it loose. Humans shout and clap their grabbers together when he carries it away. I swim below to inspect the barrier. I find the tree trunk they are trying to work free. It is a massive thing, wedged between two boulders. I put my forehead to the flatter side of one boulder and churn my flukes as hard as I can. It will not budge.

"I'll help," Deneb says. He puts his head to the boulder but cannot budge it either.

"It's too deep in the sand," I say.

I turn my flukes to the task, pumping them up and down. I make a swirl of water that stirs up the sand and carries it away. With the sand gone, we can see the trunk bending as the humans above try to pull it free. They are wedging the boulder in more tightly!

"They need to stop," I tell Deneb. "How can we get them to stop?" It would be so much better if humans could talk properly.

"Humans don't like to be wet!" Deneb says. He speeds toward the surface and leaps clear of the water right beside the humans. He flips to his back in the air and hits the water with a mighty crash. His wave splashes over the whole row of humans, and they drop the line.

"Now!" Deneb shouts.

I put my head to the boulder again and push with all my strength. It rocks. I churn my flukes harder, and it rocks some more. Deneb squeezes in beside me, and together we roll the boulder clear.

A shudder goes through the whole barrier. I feel many tiny pushes of water filtering through the thick bank of sand and mud and debris that the boulder was holding in place.

The humans shake water from their bodies. They pick up the line again. They chant again. They pull harder. The barrier shakes even more. Humans with scoopers move the sand and gravel away. The lake behind the barrier presses,

groaning, against the tangle of rubble.

"Deneb!" I shout. "Aquila! Altair! Move away!"

A jolt, almost like a sea shake, makes the barrier tremble. It creaks and shudders against the pressure of water. The largest of the trunks pulls free and unleashes the power of the river. It pushes and grinds away the sand and muck. Water swirls through a gap that widens with each beat of my racing heart. The humans drop their line. They shout. Raise their grabbers high. Leap in the air. And then the water sweeps the barrier away right beneath their feet.

"Oh, no!" Deneb groans. "Humans aren't good at being wet!"

Even as he says it, a huge surge of murky water breaks through. A channel opens. I squeeze my eyes

and breather closed as a blast of gritty water tumbles me end over end and scrapes my skin raw. I right myself and fight for breath. Where is my family? I scan the surface for fins. Deneb's pops up in front of me, and Altair's tiny fin bobs in the swirling water.

"Aquila!" I shout. I sprint to Altair's side to shelter him.

The bull sea lion roars in frustration at his interrupted feast. He calls his mothers together and swims to the nearest rocky shore. They haul their bodies out of the water and shake the silt from their fur, growling in protest. Seals follow them, and even the eagles take cover.

The gap in the rubble widens, and the river grows stronger as the enormous lake behind the barrier flows out like a mighty wind.

CHAPTER TWENTY-FIVE
KINSHIP

The salmon turn as one creature toward the call of the mountain. They fight the force of the river to answer it.

"No!" Aquila wails. "What if we never find them again?"

"If we eat them all today, we will be hungry forever after!" I shout. "We will make a wasteland of the sea!"

But Aquila cannot hear me. The hunger sickness has been chasing her for days. One good hunt cannot wipe out her fear. She charges after the salmon through the gap in the barrier. The force of the water cracks open the barrier even more; water and mud and branches and roots and entire trees sweep through.

I reach for Altair, but he is not beside me. The sea is thick with broken things, all of them moving fast. The rush of waves around me and the rolling rocks underneath me drown out everything. I lift my head above the churning water. Altair's little

fin is bobbing up and down. He is being pushed toward the islands on the other side of the channel. If the current carries him too far, I may never find him again.

"Altair!" I shout. I head toward him, but then I remember Aquila.

I cannot save them both.

Deneb rushes to my side. "Find Aquila!" he shouts. "I'll get Altair." He sprints toward the islands, calling his cousin's name.

I go after Aquila. The pressure of water beats against me as I push through the break in the barrier. Salmon flicker on either side of me, their speckled bodies emerging from the murk of muddy water and then melting out of sight. I swim with all my strength against the flood. The weight of fresh water drags me down. I keep to the surface. Logs and rocks and things I cannot name crash into me and are swept toward the sea.

Finally I glimpse the curve of Aquila's fin ahead. Ducks caught in the current squawk and flap, and then fly low over the water. A weary mink clings to a log, shaking with exhaustion. I see Aquila's fin again, near the crown of a tree—the crown of a tree! When the water drops, we will be stranded. Lost on dry land.

"Aquila!" I shout. It is no use. She cannot hear me. She does not want to hear me. The current rolls me over. Branches scrape my skin. I squeeze my eyes and breather tight and lose all sense of which way is up. My flukes hit ground and I push off, gasping and blinking mud out of my eyes. Where is Aquila? I swing my head from side to side. The tree. *There!*

"You have to let them go!" I shout. I press my body against hers. I hold her up and make her breathe.

I've done all I can for the salmon. I have to save my own family now. I spiral around Aquila, guiding her back toward the sea as quick as I can.

"We will be lost. We will be hungry!" Aquila wails.

I feel an echo of her panic in my own body. Rivers rise every year when the cold season ends and the rains are strong, but I have never seen this much fresh water. Never. The weight of it drags us down. I fight to keep my breather above water. The force of the current rolls us both over and over. My flukes scrape bottom again. My heart pounds wildly. I can feel it getting more shallow. We have to get back to the sea!

"Altair needs you!" I shout to my cousin. "Follow me!"

"Altair!" she cries. "Where is he?"

"This way!"

I swim toward the barrier with Aquila at my side. Now the press of water speeds us along. The trunk of a tree swoops past us, and one of the roots catches me as it goes by and tears open the skin on my back. The trunk rushes toward the opening in the barrier but catches on the edge.

"Quickly!" I shout. I dread being caught here, trapped, away from our family, away from the salty water of the sea. Boulders rolling along below us shake the ground. We ride through the gap like foam atop a wave.

When we break through, the salt of the sea stings in all the places where my skin is broken. But I do not care—I am free!

"Where is he?" Aquila shouts.

"Follow me!"

I head toward the islands where I last saw Deneb and Altair. I click-stream for them, but the water is a noisy jumble of debris. I jump to look above the water.

"Why did you leave him?" Aquila shouts.

Panic rises up in me like a poison. I click-stream again, but nothing orca shaped appears. I can't lose them. I can't!

"Deneb," I whisper in my own head. "Where did you go?" I remember the last time we were in danger like this, when the giant waves came. As soon as the worst part was over, he wanted to help. He wanted to make things better. I turn back to the barrier where the humans were swept away.

Two little fins are headed toward the humans.

"Deneb!" I shout.

"Altair!" Aquila races toward them.

Relief washes over me. In a moment I am beside them both. Deneb has a human draped over his nose. He nudges it toward the humans who are still on solid ground. Another human clings to Deneb's fin. Altair has the flipper of a third human in his little teeth.

"Stick! Stick!" he chants happily.

"We're helping!" Deneb says.

My brother! I am proud of him *and* relieved *and* so mad that he scared me, I could bite him! But I don't.

Aquila brushes up against Altair.

"Mama!" He drops his human to give her a nuzzle.

"I am here now," Aquila says to him. "I will always be here."

Altair snuggles up to his mother. "Me beside you," he chirps.

I swim to Deneb's side, scooping up the thrashing human that Altair dropped. I bring it to the humans, who pull it out of the water and hold it tight.

"Humans have the wrong flippers for swimming," Deneb says as we swim away. "I don't know why they go in the water at all."

The Push turns to Pull, and we let it carry us away from the churning waters of the newly opened river. We drift until we find a quiet cove, one barely touched by the destruction. We rest. Every muscle aches. I puff grit out of my breather and blink silt out of my eyes. Every torn bit of my skin stings in the clean salt of the sea. And our bellies are full. At last.

Deneb and Altair make up a game with sticks and seaweed.

"What if we can't find more salmon?" Aquila says quietly. "What if we're hungry again?"

Deneb zooms by, with Altair right behind him. "Vega knows more than she thinks she does!" he shouts.

"More, more!" Altair chirps. He waggles his flippers, as if he cannot even remember the trouble we have left behind. I do not know how little ones let go of hard times so easily. My worries stick to me like so many barnacles.

I reach out and drape a frond of kelp over Aquila's bruised sides. She sighs. We float at the surface, letting the sun warm us.

"You braved the great waves," I say. "And you lived! Your son lived! That will be a story for the ages."

Aquila brings me a long, flat blade of kelp. She draws it slowly across my cuts and bruises. The kelp takes the sting away. I thrum my contentment.

"I was wrong to doubt you before," Aquila says. She nods toward Deneb and Altair, who have moved on to a game of jump the fin. "I miss being like them. I wanted you to be a youngling for as long as you could."

I have always known that she wanted the best for me. I knew it even when I was the most crushed by her scolding. Already the sting of those harsh words is fading. Maybe in time they will become scars so small only I can see them.

We float on the tide. It has been a long time since I have felt full enough to truly rest. The afternoon shadows reach across the water, and I take in the beauty like food, like air. Even with a full belly, it fills me up to watch the blue-gray standing bird gazing into the shallows, waiting as still as a stone for a fish to come by. The shine on the water makes a rippling upside-down shadow of him. Below I see the bright purple and orange sea stars making their slow walks through the rocks and seaweeds below. So much has changed, but some things are still the same.

"Do you think we will ever find our mothers again?" Aquila says.

"I do," I say carefully, not wanting to promise. "They are looking for us too."

In my mind's eye I see the shape of my home waters. There are many rivers, large and little. Salmon come to most of them. Already I am planning the way.

"We will look for our salmon," I say. "In all the places our mothers taught us to look."

"I will never let us be hungry again," Aquila says fiercely. "Never!"

"You will be my hunter and I will be your wayfinder, and we will scour the sea to find our mothers and greatmother, our whole kinship."

"They could be anywhere," Aquila says.

"I know, but I will never give up."

I call to Deneb, and Altair tags along after him, faithful as a shadow. I glance back only for a moment. Humans are standing together on solid ground with the floodwaters going down and the salmon going up. They are reaching toward the sky; I can hear them singing.

But then I turn my eyes to the horizon and my mind to the long and perilous adventure ahead, in this wild and mysterious sea that I thought I knew so well. I am grateful and even hopeful. We swim away together—side by side and fin by fluke.

THE SOUTHERN RESIDENT KILLER WHALE COMMUNITY

Orcas—also known as killer whales—live in communities in every ocean in the world. Each community has its own prey animals and hunting strategy. This story was inspired not by a single orca but by the entire Southern Resident Killer Whale (SRKW) community of the Salish Sea. The SRKWs spend part of each year in the inland waters of the Salish Sea and part of the year along the western coast of North America. They are among the most urban of all cetaceans because the shores of the Salish Sea are home to eight million people. Orcas have been the subject

After a meal, a female orca breaches

of human art and story for many thousands of years, and SRKWs have watched the region grow from a thriving center of indigenous trade carried out in large cedar canoes to a busy international shipping region, a prime fishery, the home of naval and submarine bases, and a treasured vacation destination. They share their home with the Northern Resident Killer Whale (NRKW) community who, like their southern neighbors, eat fish—primarily salmon. Though the NRKW have much in common with the SRKW group, they do not speak the same language or socialize with one another.

A third community of killer whales shares the waters of the Salish Sea; they are called Bigg's Killer Whales or Transients. They also speak their own language and

A pod of orcas in a busy harbor-

mate only with their own. The Transients don't eat fish but instead hunt seals, porpoises, and other marine mammals— even whales.

There is also an Offshore community of killer whales, distantly related to the SRKW population but distinct in its

An orca breaches in the Salish Sea

language and hunting patterns. Little is known of this community because they range widely in the Pacific Ocean and are hard to find. They tend to travel in large groups and eat mostly squids and sharks.

Though in my story I have imagined a few moments of fellowship between these distinct orca communities, the lengths orcas go to avoid orcas from other communities is quite remarkable to those who observe them closely. Aggression between orca communities is extremely rare.

VEGA'S SALISH SEA

PACIFIC
OCEAN
⏗ The Blue
Wilderness

OLYMPIC
PENINSULA

PUGET
SOUND

SEATTLE

TACOMA

⏗ The Barrier

MT. RAINIER
The Mother
of Rivers

NISQUALLY RIVER

OLYMPIA

N

70 MILES

⏗ LABELS ARE THE ORCAS' PLACE NAMES, AS IMAGINED IN THIS BOOK

ABOUT ORCAS

LIFE • Orcas have a lifespan similar to humans. It takes them at least a dozen years to reach their adult size. They start having babies in the mid-to-late teens. They stop having babies in their forties or fifties, and we estimate they can live to be ninety, maybe even one hundred years old.

COOPERATION • Orcas are distinctive in their commitment to food sharing. Though every animal feeds its babies, few share food with extended family for their entire lives the way orcas do.

SIZE • Orcas are the largest members of the dolphin family. At 16–26 feet long, they are about as big as a triceratops.

SPEED • Orcas hunt with astonishing speed. They can sprint as fast as 30 miles per hour and dive more than 1,000 feet down, though they spend most of their time much closer to the surface. They have been known to travel as far as 100 miles in a day.

HUNT • Mammal-eating orcas can take a grown sea lion of 2,000 pounds. Sometimes they will toss a seal or porpoise they have hunted completely out of the water. Yet, for all their bulk and brawn, they are surprisingly dexterous. Orcas have been observed picking up and playing with kelp and eelgrass—or even something as small as a single feather.

ORCA COMMUNICATION

Orcas communicate with each other using calls and whistles that are produced by squeezing the air that comes through their blowholes with a pair of phonic lips, making it possible for them to talk with their mouths full. They make echolocation clicks using the same apparatus. The clicks are also shaped by the *melon*, the mass of fatty tissue that gives the orca its distinctive rounded forehead. The orca's melon acts as a sound lens. The sounds move through the melon and out like ripples on a pond. Objects in the water, such as fish, bounce the sound back to the orca. The returning sound is picked up by sound-conducting structures in the lower jaw of the orca and transmitted to the inner ear and the brain, which translates those sounds into the shape of the object ahead.

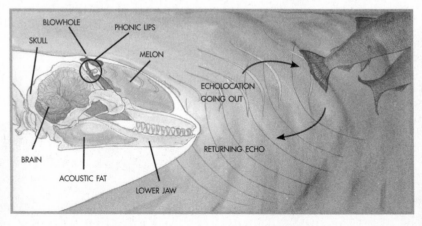

ORCA TEETH

Here is a life-sized picture of an orca tooth. The teeth are impressively sharp and can cut through the tough hides of seals and sea lions with ease. And yet in the entire history of humans living around the Salish Sea, there is no record of a wild orca ever harming a human.

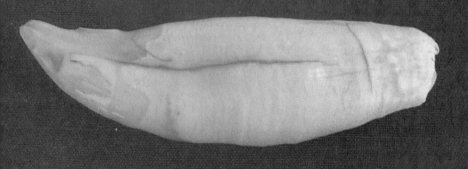

• Orcas are matrifocal, which means that their social lives are structured around the leadership of mothers. Most orcas in the southern resident community will spend the majority of their lives with their mothers—this is true for sons as well as daughters. The community relies on the matriarch's memory and navigational ability to find salmon and avoid danger.

• These extended orca families are called pods. When prey is scarce, a pod might divide into smaller groups, but when salmon are plentiful orca pods gather. Historically the SRKW pods all returned to the Salish Sea for the summer salmon runs. They greeted each other with enthusiastic chirps and whistles. They sometimes lined up and swam toward one another at first meeting, and then mingled, touching one another gently, leaping and splashing together in what appeared to be great joy. These summer meetings are less frequent now that the salmon runs are so much weaker.

SALMON

• Salmon are the keystone species of the Salish Sea. They bring nutrients from the ocean into the rivers and back to the mountain forests where they were born. They feed many animals along the way—and even the trees of the forest. Salmon depend on feeder fish like smelt and herring, who in turn rely on plankton. All these creatures rely on clean, cold, oxygen-rich water.

• The salmon runs of today contain many fewer fish than in years past, and the salmon are much smaller than they were only a few generations ago. Salmon are threatened by global warming and pollution just as orcas are. They have been overfished, and many dams block access to the streams where they once laid eggs. Careful management is needed to restore streams and rivers and allow the salmon to thrive again. Fortunately many people, particularly the indigenous people of the area, are working hard to create healthier habitats for salmon. Much work remains, but habitat restoration *is* possible.

THE FIRST NATIONS OF THE SALISH SEA

The Salish Sea was named for the language of the Coast Salish people, who live along its shores as they have for many thousands of years. More than sixty tribes in Washington and British Columbia call the Salish Sea home. Though each tribe has its own history and traditions, they share many similar cultural practices. They express a deep respect for the water and the earth, and their lives are traditionally centered around the seasonal rhythms of the returning salmon.

For the last thirty years the tribes of the Salish Sea have celebrated an annual Canoe Journey, one of the largest indigenous gatherings in North America. Canoe families from all over the Salish Sea region gather at the host nation's home waters for a celebration. They invite communities from all the canoe-making cultures of the Pacific: First Nation Canadians, Alaska Natives, Hawaiians, Maori, Papuans, and many others. The celebration takes place over several days in the summer and includes greetings in each tribe's language, feasts, singing and dancing, canoe races, and ceremonies. The communities share information both about their history and about the modern environmental problems that are putting lives in danger.

The tribes of the region have been powerful advocates for policies that would protect and restore the Salish Sea. Their scientists have provided research and innovation based in traditional resource management, which has benefitted fishery management worldwide. They have spent much of their time and resources restoring damaged rivers and removing dams that harm salmon. Many of these tribes count the orcas as their kin; the orcas are fortunate to have such skilled advocates.

THE HABITATS OF THE SALISH SEA REGION

Vega and Deneb traveled hundreds of miles through the waterways, inlets, and coves of the Salish Sea; over the edge of the continental shelf; and into the deep ocean before returning to their home waters.

INLAND SEA

The **Salish Sea** is one of the largest and most biologically diverse inland seas in the world. It lies along the coast of Washington State in the US and British Columbia in Canada. The sea contains 419 islands and more than 4,600 miles of coastline. It gets its name from the Coast Salish tribes who have always lived along its shores since the glaciers of the last ice age retreated, leaving deep fjords, whaleback-shaped islands, and a network of rivers that bring a steady supply of nutrient-rich silt to the sea. Those nutrients form the base of a food web that includes thousands of species of marine invertebrates, fish, birds, and mammals, including the eight million humans who live along its shores.

The **giant Pacific octopus** is the largest octopus in the world. It can grow to be almost 30 feet from the tip of one tentacle to another. The suckers on its eight legs are used to grip things and also for tasting and smelling. It has three hearts and nine brains—a main central brain and one in each leg. Octopuses are highly intelligent, brilliant at camouflage, and live almost entirely solitary lives.

The **gray whale** is a baleen whale, meaning that it feeds by filtering its food through long baleen plates in its mouth. Gray whales specialize in scooping up amphipods (small crustaceans) from the mud and silt of the sea floor. They migrate every year from their winter feeding grounds in the Arctic to their summer calving lagoons in Baja California.

At 10,000 to 12,000 miles, it is one of the longest mammal migration routes in the world. Because gray whales migrate close to the shore, their heart-shaped blows are easily seen from the beach. Gray whales are a conservation success story; during the height of commercial whaling they numbered less than two thousand. But now they are more than 25,000 strong and are no longer on the endangered species list.

Common murres live most of their lives at sea. They are clumsy fliers but incredibly nimble underwater as they hunt for a wide variety of small fish, including herring, anchovy, and smelt. Murres come ashore only once in the spring, when each pair lays a single egg. The murres crowd together on steep cliffs and bare rocks. They do not build actual nests but lay their speckled eggs directly on the rocks. The eggs are pointy on one end, so that they roll in a circle when bumped rather than rolling off the edge of the cliff.

Herring, anchovies, smelt, and **sardines** are all similar-looking, crayon-sized fish that travel in large schools. They are called forage fish because they provide food for larger fish, such as salmon and halibut; seabirds, such as murres and puffins; and marine mammals, including seals, porpoises, and whales—and humans too. Because they are food for so many other creatures, their survival strategy is to lay epic quantities of eggs.

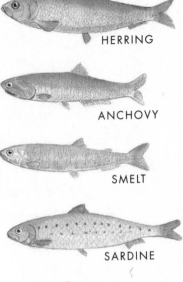

HERRING

ANCHOVY

SMELT

SARDINE

Eelgrass meadows grow in estuaries where fresh and salt water mix. Their roots help stabilize sandy and muddy bottoms. They provide food for birds, a nesting place for the eggs of many small feeder fish, and a home to crabs, sea stars, clams, snails, anemones, and sea urchins. And they provide a safe place with plenty of food for young salmon to transition from their freshwater birthplaces to the ocean. Eelgrass can help reduce the acidification of the ocean, and like rainforests, it absorbs carbon dioxide to combat global warming.

CONTINENTAL SHELF

The **Olympic Coast National Marine Sanctuary** encompasses the mouth of the Salish Sea and extends about 100 miles along an undeveloped stretch of Washington shore. It reaches westward 25 to 50 miles, to the edge of the continental shelf, and contains 600 small islands, emergent rocks, and arches. These tiny refuges provide resting spots for seals, sea lions, and millions of birds. The North Pacific is colder and less salty than the North Atlantic. It is well known for rough seas and big waves. The continental slope is very steep here. Wind and ocean currents bring upwellings of nutrient-rich cold water from the deep. This upwelling feeds plankton, which become food for an abundance of fish, birds, and marine mammals.

Mussels are a type of shellfish that cling to the rocky shorelines. They live in the intertidal zone, so when the tide is ebbing they close their shells tightly to keep from drying out and to protect themselves from predators like otters, sea stars, raccoons, and humans. Like clams and barnacles, they are filter feeders, drawing water into their bodies and filtering out plankton to eat. A mussel can filter a bathtub full of water every day, which means that they play a key role in keeping our seas and oceans clean. But it also means that pollutants in the water can accumulate in the mussels, sending those poisons up the food web.

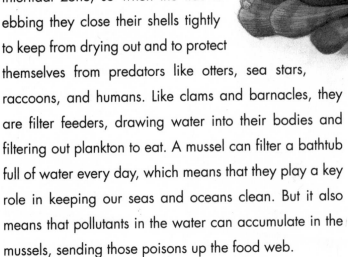

Bull kelp is one of the fastest-growing plants in the ocean. It starts as a tiny spore and can grow as much as 10 inches a day, reaching a height of 30 to 60 feet by midsummer. A holdfast anchors it to the bottom, and a bulb at the top of the thick and flexible stem floats on the surface. Many long, flat blades attach to the bulb. Forests of bull kelp and giant kelp provide important shelter for fish, crabs, sea stars, and sea urchins. Seals and sea otters also like to hide in kelp beds.

Gulls are one of the must numerous birds of both the Pacific and Atlantic coasts. They often nest in large and noisy colonies. Gulls are opportunistic feeders—they have a hugely varied diet that they gather both at sea and onshore. It includes small fish, mollusks, crustaceans, insects, eggs, and even smaller birds. They are also well-known consumers of dropped French fries and other human-generated garbage.

Sea otters can spend their entire lives in the ocean, and yet their skin never gets wet, because they have the most dense fur of any animal on earth—about a million hairs per square inch of skin. The air trapped in their fur keeps otters warm and buoyant. They are also one of the very few animals to use tools. Much of their food—sea urchins, crabs, clams, mussels, abalone, and snails—has a shell, so they use rocks to break shellfish free and then use a rock again to break open the shells to eat the meat inside.

Like all the other members of the weasel family, sea otters have five toes on each paw, and they catch fish with their paws and not their mouths.

Harbor seals, like sea otters, were once hunted to near-extinction. But the Marine Mammal Protection Act passed in 1972 has helped them recover to a stable population. Harbor seals spend about half of their time on land—resting, birthing pups, and molting. Though most of their hunting for food only requires short and shallow dives, harbor seals can go as deep as 1500 feet and stay down for 30 minutes. In a deep dive, a seal slows its heart down to only a few beats per minute, which helps conserve oxygen. It then uses the oxygen stored in its muscles.

OPEN OCEAN

The **open ocean** is also called the **pelagic zone**. It is the area beyond the coast and the continental shelf, where the water becomes much deeper and the number and variety of living creatures decreases dramatically.

Krill are not much to look at—pink, opaque, and the size and weight of a paper clip, they spend their lives in a swarm, eating phytoplankton. But if you put all the krill in the world on one end of a balance scale and all the humans on the other, the krill would weigh more. There are 85 different species, and most are bioluminescent, meaning that they glow in the dark. Krill are a vital source of food for whales, penguins, seabirds, fish, and seals. Like eelgrass, they play a huge role in taking carbon out of the atmosphere and depositing it on the ocean floor, making them tiny heroes in the fight against global warming.

Phytoplankton are microscopic plants and **zooplankton** are microscopic animals. All together, **plankton** are the most numerous creatures in the world. They are the basis of the food chain of every ocean, feeding the smallest animals, which in turn feed larger ones. Half the world's oxygen comes from photosynthesis done by phytoplankton. Much of the world's oil and natural gas is made up of decayed plankton remains.

Bigeye thresher sharks have tails that are as long as their whole bodies. They use the tails to stun fish, often several at once, making them easier to catch and eat. Threshers have smaller mouths than most sharks, but they have much larger than normal eyes, to help them hunt at night. They eat fish, little ones like sardines and others as big as a tuna. They also eat squid. Though we only know a little bit about the offshore community of orcas in the North Pacific, we do know they eat sharks and squid.

Laysan albatrosses nest on islands in the Pacific, especially the Hawaiian Islands, and they travel all over the north Pacific, sometimes flying more than 300 miles in a day. Their wingspan of almost seven feet makes it possible for them to soar for hours without flapping their wings. In calm weather they float on the surface of the ocean to catch fish and squid, but when the winds are strong, they can snap up a meal in flight. They are one of only a few animals who can drink salt water without getting dehydrated. Albatrosses live unusually long lives. They are not fully grown until they are 8 or 9 years old and they can live to be 65.

Blue whales are the largest animals in the world; a blue whale's tongue weighs as much as an elephant and its heart is the size of a car. And yet they survive on one of the smallest animals—krill. Blue whales swim, alone or in pairs, in every ocean except for the Arctic. They can live as long as 90 years. They are also the loudest creature on earth—in good conditions blue whales can hear one another from 1,000 miles away.

DANGERS IN THE SALISH SEA

Although no animals hunt and eat orcas, there are many threats to orcas' survival. From 1964 to 1976, more than 200 orcas in the Salish Sea were put through the stress of capture, some of them more than once. This led to the deaths of at least a dozen whales. More than 50 others were sold to marine entertainment parks around the world. Those captured would have been the matriarchs of today. The loss of their knowledge and the babies they would have mothered has made the lives of the current community extremely challenging.

Another stress on the orcas is pollution. Runoff from roads, cities, industries, mines, and farms—as well as fuel leakage from boats—all send toxins into the water. The toxins are absorbed into the plants and planktons of the sea and work their way up the food chain so that the apex predators—orcas, seals, sea lions, and eagles—carry the heaviest toxic load. Ordinarily orcas' bodies absorb a toxin and store it in their blubber, where it causes them little harm. But when food is scarce and the orcas start to live off the energy reserve in their blubber, the toxins enter their bloodstream and make them sick. The toxins, combined with a dramatic decrease in the number of salmon returning to the Salish Sea, are part of the reason so many orca calves are stillborn or die in the first few months of life. Abandoned fishing gear and plastic garbage also threaten animals in all the world's oceans.

Noise is a kind of pollution, too. Because orcas rely on echolocation, the noise from ship traffic makes it harder for them to hunt and may cause them to travel farther and forage less. Fortunately, there are solutions to ship noise. Slowing down in the presence of whales and orcas and keeping distance from them reduces the pressure of noise pollution. Efforts are underway to convert some ferries to electricity, which will reduce both their noise and their carbon footprint.

The world's oceans are on the front lines of the war against global warming. Warmer water holds less oxygen. Even a small increase in temperature affects the whole food chain. For orcas, salmon are the key component of the food chain. The biggest problem orcas face, by far, is the lack of salmon. Salmon runs are down 60–90 percent in recent years. And salmon today are half the size they once were, but they still take the same amount of energy to hunt.

HOW CAN I HELP THE ORCAS?

In order to thrive, orcas require clean, cold, quiet water and a healthy food chain. Though the SRKW are under threat from many sources, there is much that can be done to help them. It is already illegal to hunt or capture orcas or any other marine mammal in US waters. The Marine Mammal Protection Act was passed in 1972 with the help of schoolchildren who wrote their members of Congress to demand action. Any person can raise their voice to ask for change. Any person can change their behavior to make the world better. Here are some things you can do to help protect the Salish Sea and every river and sea in the entire world:

1. Use less energy. Global warming is rooted in the burning of fossil fuels. Try to use less fuel by walking, biking, or skating instead of riding in a car. Wear something warm instead of turning up the heat. Turn off lights and electronics when you are not using them.

2. Use less stuff, and recycle. Plastic is dangerous in the oceans. It entangles and chokes sea life, and it eventually breaks down into tiny bits that are swallowed. Reuse plastic items like water bottles and bags or use alternatives.

3. Learn about your local ecosystem. You'll be most effective when you advocate close to home, and there is plenty to do in your own backyard.

4. Raise your voice. Write letters to local news channels and to your representatives in Congress. You have a right to speak to people in power and to protest when their actions are dangerous. The creatures and plants of the Earth need your voice.

5. Respect your local indigenous community and learn from their environmental research and teachings. Many of America's strongest environmental initiatives have been rooted in and led by indigenous communities.

6. Believe that the problems of global warming and pollution can be solved. When I was a child, I never saw an eagle. Not once. But we learned that the pesticide DDT was poisoning the raptors of the world (and also insects, fish, amphibians, other birds, and people) and so we stopped using DDT. Slowly the food chain got healthier, and now I see eagles all the time—and hawks and osprey and falcons, too.

Author's Note

As I write this story, the Southern Resident Killer Whales who inspired it are under threat like never before. Their numbers have dropped to one of the lowest points in recorded history. Pollution and ship noise and the lack of salmon have pushed these beautiful animals to the brink. Even more concerning, the very forces of climate change and pollution that hurt orcas are just as dangerous to humans. But I also know that the darkest and most difficult times in our history have been the times when people have been their bravest and their most innovative.

Every problem facing our orcas in the Salish Sea has a solution. Some are already being put in place. Older ferries are being replaced by cleaner, quieter electric ferries. The Elwha was once a dead river, but dams have been removed and salmon are now spawning in that river again. New rules have forced boats to go slowly when whales are present, so that they don't make as much noise. The Lummi Nation has used its treaty-protected fishing rights to prevent the largest coal terminal in North

America from being placed in the Salish Sea.

Our oceans are on the front line of the war against global warming. Restoring our planet and reversing climate change will be the fight of our lives. I am inspired every day by the activism of my young readers. I'm confident that together we can heal our world and all its waters.

Artist's Note

When I try to describe something clearly in a drawing, I always notice new details. Drawing carefully allows me to learn more about an organism, and I learned so much about the Salish Sea ecosystem while illustrating this story. I would encourage young artists, scientists, and others with a genuine curiosity for the world to keep a pencil and sketchbook on their journeys (down the road or across the globe). Drawing is a way to teach yourself, through observation, more about the world around you.

Resources for Young Readers

Lindstrom, Carole and Michaela Goade, illus., *We Are Water Protectors*. New York: Roaring Brook Press, Macmillan Publishers, 2020.

Marks, Johnny and Hans Chester, David Katzeek, Nora Dauenhauer, and Richard Dauenhauer, eds., and Michaela Goade, illus. *Shanyaak'utlaax Salmon Boy*. Baby Raven Reads Series. Juneau, AK: Sealaska Heritage Institute, 2017. This is a bilingual edition, published in English and Tlingit.

McAllister, Ian, and Nicholas Read. *The Seal Garden*. Vancouver, BC: Orca Book Publishers, 2018.

McAllister, Ian, and Nicholas Read. *A Whale's World*. Vancouver, BC: Orca Book Publishers, 2018.

Valice, Kim Perez. *The Orca Scientists*. Scientists in the Field Series. Boston: HMH Books for Young Readers, 2018.

Vickers, Roy Henry and Robert Budd. *Orca Chief*. Madiera Park, BC: Harbour Publishing, 2015.

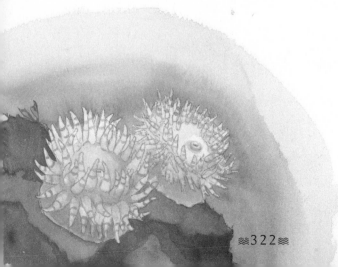

General Resources

Benedict, Audrey DeLella and Joseph K Gaydos. *The Salish Sea: Jewel of the Pacific Northwest.* Seattle: Sasquatch Books, 2015.

Safina, Carl. *Beyond Words: What Animals Think and Feel.* New York: Henry Holt and Co/Picador, 2015.

Thompson, Jerry. *Cascadia's Fault: The Coming Earthquake and Tsunami That Could Devastate North America.* Berkeley, CA: Counterpoint Press, 2011.

The Center for Whale Research tracks orcas in the Salish Sea and posts pictures of the encounters on its website.
https://www.whaleresearch.com

The SeaDoc Society has a short video series called Salish Sea Wild; perfect for use in the classroom.
https://www.seadocsociety.org/salish-sea-wild

The NOAA Fisheries website contains a wealth of information about the habitats and species of the ocean, including a series on how orcas use echolocation to hunt.
https://www.fisheries.noaa.gov

The Discovery of Sound in the Sea website has a fascinating audio gallery of maritime sounds.
https://dosits.org/galleries/audio-gallery/audio-gallery-summary/

Acknowledgments

Every story is a collaboration. I am especially grateful to my research partner, who hiked with me to the end of the continent, paddled through choppy seas, watched sea otters by moonlight, and drew every single amazing illustration in this book. Thank you, Lindsay Moore! I met and spoke with so many citizens of the Salish Sea, who shared their stories and their love of the Southern Resident Killer Whale community with me. I could never name them all, but I am especially grateful for Lois Landgrebe, Tulalip storyteller and teacher of the Lushootseed language; and Katie Jones, educator and outreach manager for the Center for Whale Research. Cheers to my wonderful editor, Virginia Duncan, and the whole team at Greenwillow, including Sylvie Le Floc'h, Tim Smith, Lois Adams, Laaren Brown, Robert Imfeld, Mikayla Lawrence, and Arianna Robinson. My tenacious and talented agent, Fiona Kenshole of Transatlantic Agency, is the wizard of words who makes all this possible. And as always, I'm grateful to my family, who have helped me find my way and traveled at my side, mile after literary mile.

The author (right) and artist in the Salish Sea